Lost

Lost

Eve Ainsworth

SCHOLASTIC

Scholastic Children's Books
An imprint of Scholastic Ltd
Euston House, 24 Eversholt Street, London, NW1 1DB, UK
Registered office: Westfield Road, Southam, Warwickshire, CV47 0RA
SCHOLASTIC and associated logos are trademarks and/or
registered trademarks of Scholastic Inc.

First published in the UK by Scholastic Ltd, 2019

Text copyright © Eve Ainsworth, 2019

The right of Eve Ainsworth to be identified as the
author of this work has been asserted.

ISBN 978 1407 18544 6

A CIP catalogue record for this book
is available from the British Library.

Printed by CPI Group (UK) Ltd, Croydon, CR0 4YY
Papers used by Scholastic Children's Books are made
from wood grown in sustainable forests.

13 5 7 9 10 8 6 4 2

To Ethan, my own football star.
I couldn't be prouder, Love you for ever x

She took his hand, grubby and small, and squeezed it tightly in hers. It was crisp day, and the air pinched at their faces. There was a scent of salt around them, a freshness that both caught their breath and caught in their throats.

They walked the usual way, turning right at the newsagent and looping around it at a slow, careful pace. His steps were clumsy and he stopped often to point out the things that caught his eye. A silver slug trail. A pretty stone. A discarded crisp packet. Nothing of significance, but to him they were tiny pieces of wonder. He was five years old and the world was beautiful.

She didn't mind his slow pace. She was rarely in a rush. Her words were soft, thoughtful. She praised him often, touched his hair, stroked his face, squeezed his fingers. Her hands were gentle against his, her nails long and painted red. Always red. Always vivid against his white skin.

They headed towards their favourite point. Just as the road turned into the promenade, they would cross and stand by the railings. Here they had the best view, right out to sea and to the long outstretched finger of the pier on their left.

They went there again today and stood back a little from the edge of the rails – her eyes were darting, looking across the shore and over the wild waves. Her finger went towards her lips. She was always looking. She told him she was waiting for the seagulls to come. Most people hated them, but not her. She loved their sound. She said their cries were like the music of the sea.

It was quiet today, no one around at all. She began to sing softly under her breath, just broken bits of tunes from the radio. Familiar lyrics that curled comfortably into his brain. Other times she would sing different, older songs. Songs that she said her own mother had sung to her. She looked sad then. He knew that her mum had died. He knew that she only had them now.

Her voice caught gently in the breeze.

"In Dublin's fair city,
Where the girls are so pretty,
I first set my eyes on sweet Molly Malone,

As she wheeled her wheelbarrow,
Through streets broad and narrow,
Crying, 'Cockles and mussels, alive, alive, oh!'
'Alive, alive, oh,
Alive, alive, oh,'
Crying, 'Cockles and mussels, alive, alive, oh.'"

He lifted his head and watched her. She seemed so happy and peaceful, the sun catching the brightness of her curls, her eyes sparkling in the light as she smiled back down at him.

She ran her hand through his unruly hair.

"You'll always be my special boy," she said.

He nodded. He knew it was true. He pushed himself up close beside her and they didn't move. The light breeze continued to whip around them, so gently it was as if they were both being stroked.

It was perfect. It was just how he always wanted it to be.

Chapter One

Seven o'clock in the morning and the house was an empty shell. The door to Dad's room stood open, like a hungry gaping mouth. The bed was neatly made, and everything was tidied away just as it should be. I stood for a moment at the door, looking in, feeling that heavy dread coiled inside my stomach. It was stupid. I knew he had to leave early today but it didn't stop the uneasy feeling, the same old worry drip-feeding into my gut. The house was full of echoes and space and I didn't like it.

In fact, I hated it.

There is something about this house when it's empty. It is hard to describe but it always unsettles me – like bony fingers scratching at the back of my neck, daring me to turn around and look deep into the shadows to see the things I am afraid to see. The things that are no longer there.

The missing stuff.

The gaps.

It makes me want to be a little kid again, run under the bed and hide. Or to get far away and not be here at all. It was too still. I wanted noise, a little bit of madness.

I just wanted something else.

I got dressed and went downstairs. The doors sat closed. Shadows drifted in the corners and around the edges. I swear it never used to be this cold and dark. He'd left out my breakfast as usual. A packet of cereal and a bowl. No note, of course. I could see his unfinished mug of coffee on the drainer. Other than that, the kitchen was completely tidy – untouched, almost. Unlived-in. I glanced at the cereal for a second, wondering if I could be bothered to eat, but my stomach felt too tight and small. I scanned the room, considering the options – the small loaf of bread poking out of the bread bin, the few remaining biscuits in the jar. It was no use. I needed to get out of there.

I picked up my bag, plucked the keys from the

bowl in the hall and slammed out of the front door. I tried to ignore the overgrown grass and Dad's neglected bike leaning against the fence. It never used to be like this, and if I got away from here and concentrated really hard, I could pretend it still wasn't.

Despite my thoughts, my body was under protest as I dragged it down the path that winds along the side of our house. I guess most of me still wanted to be in bed. In truth, I was probably mad to be out of the house so early. But what choice did I have? Stay inside, in there, alone, or be outside, away from it all. I felt like a ghost walking in the weak morning light. It was still so dark. My school bag pulled hard on my muscles where I'd slung it over my shoulder. There was no one else around – no dog walkers, not even that mad jogger who lives at the other end of the road. I breathed in hard, taking in large lungfuls of air, trying to wake myself. The autumn air was sharp and crisp. The leaves crunched under my feet, breaking into dust.

Dust to dust. . .

The path turned a sharp left behind the house and followed a muddy track between bushes and tall, spindly trees. I could walk this in the pitch black and not fall, it is so familiar to me. Every stone, every dip, every tree root. I pushed up, shoving aside the overgrown branches. The route runs alongside the allotments and was dead at that time of morning – although I was pretty sure I could see some movement on the patch in the far corner. Maybe I wasn't the only weirdo up and about.

On the opposite side of the path is the small park for kids. My eyes scanned the fenced area quickly: the small blue slide, the baby swings, the climbing frame that had once seemed impossibly tall. I turned my head away. I'd not been in that place for years. It was part of the past. I reached the small, rotting stile at the end of the path, stumbling over it with my bag banging heavily against my side. The ground was pretty boggy on the other side and I cursed under my breath as my foot planted nicely into a huge muddy puddle. But I carried on nonetheless, ploughing ahead uphill, across the field, walking faster. I preferred this route. OK, it was a little longer, but it was more interesting. And quieter. I might bump into the occasional dog-walker, but that would be about it. And thankfully none of them would be interested in speaking to me.

At the top, the slope flattened into the playing

field, and I stopped to take a few deep breaths. The old goalposts stood at the far side. This was the place where we always went to play. Actually, the others still go there. Why wouldn't they? Nothing has changed for them. I remembered what it felt like to just turn up here, dump my stuff and throw myself into a game.

Something tugged at my stomach, and I blinked hard. I quickly turned the other way. I could see it now.

The sea.

I kept walking till I was clear of the grass and on the promenade. The road was practically empty as I crossed it and made my way over to the railings and along to the furthest blue bench, the one nearest the broken-down pier that stretches out to sea. This was my place. *Our* place. Where we'd always gone.

Me and Mum.

She said it was a tiny piece of paradise. Maybe that was going too far, but it *was* special. To us, anyway. The grey, rolling waves crashed in welcome; the salt air whipped around me, freezing my face and numbing my lips. It was an odd mixture of quiet and noisy there. You could be totally alone, and yet you weren't. The sea has a way of making you feel part of it.

I felt myself relax.

Carefully I leant up against the railings. The iron was cool and hard against my back. Now I could really concentrate. I could really listen. And they were calling, of course – the birds. And today I was determined to be there. To be with them again.

I lifted my head and waited.

They came – slowly at first, but soon within my sight: swooping, shrieking seagulls. They didn't seem to mind me. One even landed a few metres away, his wings stretched out wide in a crooked kind of greeting. His head tilted slightly and his beady eyes regarded me with curiosity.

"Morning," I whispered, my words seeming to fizz on the cold air. "It's good to see you, mate."

I swear he tipped his head a little more, his beak turning towards me. Was I going mad?

"She always said—"

"Who are you talking to?"

I froze. For the briefest of moments, that voice threw me. It was too familiar. I shifted position, turned around. But of course it wasn't her. It was someone else – just some girl, standing there staring, her hand resting against the lamp post behind me. I definitely didn't recognize her. She looked young, much younger than me. And she was so thin she could've blended into the railings I was standing by. Her dark hair was wild and the wind whipped it around her pale, white face, and around her darkly made-up eyes. She had a bright, red smile. Her eyes sparkled as she caught my gaze.

"Were you talking to yourself?" she asked again bluntly. Her voice was loud against the breeze.

I blinked. The seagull had gone now, stupid traitor, so it obviously looked like I had been talking to myself. Mind you, was it any better to admit that I had been whispering to a manky old bird?

"What's it got to do with you?" I said, getting up quickly. I didn't need this. I didn't want anyone else around. Why was she even here at this hour? It was so early. Too early for people like her. I came here at this time for that very reason, because I didn't want to see anyone. I didn't want to be bothered.

"Bit weird, that's all. . ." she muttered.

I glared back at her. Was she for real? Staring at me like that, while she was dressed in some shabby grey T-shirt and shapeless jeans. She looked like she'd dug her clothes out of a bin. And wasn't she cold? She didn't even have a coat on. I flinched. Was she OK?

But I didn't have time for this. Not now. I needed

to be on my own. I shook my head slowly, hitching my bag over my shoulder.

"So why are you here?" she said.

"I just am ... no reason..."

"Nice." She grinned. "You're dead friendly, you are."

I shrugged. "Sorry..."

I started to move away. "I'm not weird," I said as I passed her. After all, I wasn't the one standing in the cold spying on other people. I wasn't the one who needed to brush my hair. And I wasn't the one dressed for summer on an icy morning.

"Hey!" she shouted, but I didn't want to talk to her. I didn't want *anyone*. I only wanted the seagull and she had scared it away.

So, thanks for that.

He was too excited, dressed in his new football kit. He kicked a cushion across the floor, watching it skid and turn. He loved his new boots the best. They were yellow and green and had been his favourite ones in the shop. He had got them as a reward for his hat trick last week. His mum always knew which ones he liked the most. She liked treating him.

"Hey watch it, Ronaldo!" she laughed. "I don't want you smashing up the house."

She was gathering up his bag, his drink, his shin pads. Outside it was pouring hard with rain, but neither of them cared.

"Let's go!" she yelled.

They ran to the car, giggling and shrieking as the rain splattered against their faces. She moaned about the weather making her hair even more "wild", but her complaints didn't seem that real. She was smiling all the time. On the short drive he couldn't stop talking. What would this team be like? Was he good enough to play for them? What if he played badly? His mum simply smiled at him through the rear-view mirror.

"You'll be fine," she said. "You're my little star."

They parked up and strode across the muddy field towards a large man with a red, ruddy face. He stepped forwards and held out his hand for shaking.

"Alfie. I've heard good things about you. Your mum says you have quite a talent."

He looked up. His mum was beaming. She ruffled his hair.

"He's only eight but he's been playing above his age for two years now at Rushfield. But it's time for new challenges. I've heard this is the best team."

The man grinned. "Indeed. And we need a good midfielder."

"Is Dad not coming?" Alfie asked her.

She shook her head. "He has to work. But he's dead proud too." She leant in close "But not as proud as me," she whispered in his ear.

"Come on," said his new coach. "I'll introduce you to the rest of the team."

He paused, feeling that little twist of anxiety that often pulled him back.

Could he really do this?

He looked back at his mum and she just nodded gently.

"It'll be fine, Alfie. I'm here. I'm not leaving you."

She was right. Of course she was right. He knew that she would be watching him the whole time.

She wasn't going anywhere.

Chapter Two

I walked into school the usual way, not even bothering to knock for Ben. He's always late, anyway. And besides, I didn't mind being on my own. I was still tired and not in the mood to talk. My run-in with that girl had wound me up. I wished she hadn't caught me talking to myself. I'd not seen her around here before, but it's a small town. What if she was some new kid? Someone starting off rumours about me was all I needed.

Hey, have you heard? Alfie talks to himself.

And, worse than that, he talks to birds. What a freak.

I shook the thoughts away. Hopefully she was no one. Hopefully I'd never see her again. As I passed through the main gates, my phone buzzed. The usual, predictable text from Dad.

Have a good day. See you at 4. Are you doing footie later?

No, Dad, I'm not doing footie later. I haven't done footie for months. I keep telling you this...

I didn't answer him – there was no point; he never listens. I turned my phone off and walked into the building with my head low and my body braced for another day. I don't hate school. I used to *really* like it. And I guess in some ways I still do even though there are a few idiots there. Quite a few idiots, in fact. But I find it so much harder to concentrate now. My mind keeps flicking backwards, and stuff trickles in, even though I fight against it. When it gets bad – really bad – I don't want to be there at all. Everything feels so meaningless. What is the point of school when life is so rubbish anyway? People keep telling you that you can make your life better, when in actual fact you have no control over most of it.

It's hard just carrying on. Pretending to be normal like the rest of them even though I am far from normal now. The idiots leave me alone, but only because they feel sorry for me. In some ways that's worse, isn't it? Because I never asked for their pity.

I never wanted that.

In maths I sat at the back, staring at the line of numbers, watching as they blurred in front of me. It was quite a trick. Maths is meant to be my best subject, but that seems like a cruel joke at the moment. I can barely remember how to add up now.

Behind me, I could hear Cole and Kayden whispering about football or girls or something else pointless. Actually, it wasn't even whispering, they were practically shouting, but no one seemed that bothered. We had some meek cover teacher, a blonde woman with a wispy face and watery eyes. She kept glancing over at our tables, as if a look would be enough to stop them, which only made Cole laugh as he leant back in his chair. But when he lost his balance and ended up kicking my chair, the jolt shuddered through my entire body. I slammed down my pen and turned around.

"Seriously?" I hissed.

Cole's eyes widened. He is proper annoying, always acting like he owns the school or something.

He's the same on the football pitch. He sat forward and flashed me one of his wide, cheesy grins.

"Sorry, Alfie mate. Did I knock you?"

"Yeah, actually. You did."

Kayden was still giggling, his red cheeks looking ready to explode. Like Cole, he thinks he is fit, but the girls only like him because of his reputation. It's pathetic.

"Alfie! Chill!" he said, his hands up in mock defence as he flashed Cole a side glance and sniggered.

"I can't concentrate with you two messing about," I said.

Then I saw it. The sparkle of malice dancing in their eyes. Cole nudged Kayden and snorted. They both wanted to say it. They both wanted to rib me for actually caring. For being a whiney little swot.

But they didn't. They just stared back at me. Fake innocent expressions pasted on their faces. I wanted to punch them both.

Cole moved back again and his face switched to neutral.

"I'm sorry, mate," he said softly.

But I kept staring at them, willing them to say more – to say what they really wanted to.

C'mon lads. You never used to be this tame. Remember how we'd tear into each other? You'd call me every name you wanted. You'd properly roast me. Don't let me off now.

But they just kept staring at me with their calm little faces. Trying to be nice. Trying to do the right thing. I turned back to my work, staring once again at the blurred numbers in front of me. Numbers that were not going to work for me today.

I wasn't going to get anything done. And I still thought they were complete idiots.

If I could, I would rip away this cotton wool that is wrapped around me, tear it into shreds and ram it down someone's throat. I didn't ask for *any* of this. I don't want any special treatment. I want to be the same as before. Why do they think they are helping me? Dad, my teachers, Cole and the rest of them, all acting like I'm some kind of diseased animal. Avoiding me – being kind when they never would have been before.

Treating me like this doesn't help – it doesn't stop the stuff inside me. It just means everyone acts differently. And that's worse. Much worse.

Stop being kind.

Please.

I really hate it.

Being kind is the worst thing you can do.

Because how can I move forward when it feels like everyone is holding me back?

There is one person who I could rely on treat me the same, though. One person who keeps me sane, although saying that feels kind of ironic because most days he drives me bloody nuts too.

Ben.

"All right, loser?" he said, as he threw his backpack across the table and sat down heavily on the seat in front of me in the lunch hall. He let out a loud sigh, just in case I hadn't already noticed him.

"I seriously think my life is over," he said, in a kind of matter-of-fact tone, like he'd just told me the weather forecast. I stared back at him. He looked well over the top today, even for him. His usually spiked-up quiff was bright purple and somehow even higher than ever, and I think he had eyeliner on too, but I couldn't be sure.

"Man, your hair. What the hell?"

He reached up and touched his head like he'd forgotten it was there, then laughed.

"Oh yeah, I nicked Lara's dye. She's going to kill me. What do you think?"

I stared at it some more. "It's pretty bright. Haven't school said anything?"

Ben shrugged. "Malone noticed it today in registration, but he's a bit preoccupied with his divorce."

"He's getting divorced?"

"Oh yeah. Everyone knows that. He burst into tears during music last week. Apparently, the song they were doing reminded him of his wife." Ben sniggered, opening up his bag. "It was a Lady Gaga one, so that was a bit tragic. It makes you wonder, really. . ."

I bit into my sandwich. "So, what's this about your life being over?"

Ben slammed his empty crisp packet down in emphasis. "Alf, man, it is. I think I'm in love."

"Oh, really? Who is it this time?"

I swear Ben has this thing about being in love, because he is "in love" most days. Then the wind changes and he starts obsessing about someone else. He has the attention span of a bug.

"Becky Collins."

I stopped eating. "What, in year eleven? You're joking?"

"No, I'm not. She's proper fit—"

"And she's older than you. And she's dating Sam Jarvis."

"Nah, apparently she dumped him last week. Anyway, she smiled at me today."

I sighed. "She smiles at *everyone*, mate. She's like that."

"Well . . . I like her," he said, as he leant in towards me. "And I have a feeling I should be with an older woman. I'm that sort of person."

"Probably best to keep this obsession to yourself, though," I said, staring back at him.

He scrunched up his crisp packet and shoved it back into his bag. "It's not an obsession. But you're probably right. I don't want *everyone* knowing. . ."

Ben studied me for a second, a serious look passing across his face. But he seemed to shake it away with a nod.

"How was it today?" he said finally.

"Fine, like always."

"And your dad?"

"Fine."

Like always.

*

I left school dead on the bell, ploughing out of my final lesson and through the crowds before anyone could stop me. I didn't want to be caught up in any after-school stuff. I just wanted to get home. My head felt full up, but it wasn't full of school, it was full of other things. Perhaps that's the problem. There isn't any room left in there. It even felt heavy as I walked, as if it took effort just to keep it upright. I glanced over at the reception as I left. I like Susan, the woman who worked there – she is always dead friendly to me. Today she was chatting to Becky Collins, who I found myself studying as I passed. I don't know if she could feel my eyes on her, but she turned around.

"Hey, Alfie! You OK? Have a good one."

I still couldn't see why Ben was bothering with her. She is totally out of his league.

"Thanks, Becs," I muttered, as my eyes looked past her, towards the back room behind reception – the place where visitors wait before they see the head teacher.

Without even realizing it I slowed my pace, almost stopping.

The girl was there – the one from this morning – sitting skinny and pale on a chair, next to a larger woman with one small boy on her lap and a pram in front of her. The woman was talking loudly and jiggling the kid around a lot.

The girl looked up and caught me staring at her, but she held my gaze, her eyes hard.

The mum was still talking, actually she was shouting at the boy on her lap, but the girl didn't look away.

I did.

He'd spent ages on it, carefully thinking about each individual brick before pushing them on to the bright green base. It had to be just right. The windows needed to line up perfectly, the door needed to be large and right in the middle. He wasn't going to rush this time. She had liked the last one, but not enough. This one had to make her really happy.

It had to be like they had talked about: perfect.

He had found a tiny tree, forgotten and misshapen at the bottom of the box. His fingers stroked the flattened plastic. It didn't matter — maybe it looked like the wind had flattened the branches. He fixed it to the corner of his model, but, no, there was something wrong. A dark stain at the bottom of the tree — a black mark like a tiny thumbprint on it. What was it? Ink?

It made him think of the tree near the beach. The

lightning tree, completely scorched and black, yet still standing upright, looking like its dark neck was tipping towards the sun, begging to be revived. He'd always stare up at it and imagine what it had been like before the bolt had struck. He wondered if it had hurt. Did it feel the blaze of fire rip through its bark? Did the sparks ignite its leaves and burn them instantly? Did it suffer?

He studied his plastic tree a little longer before plucking it away from the base and carefully returning it to the box. It was spoilt now. He wanted to forget about it, pretend he hadn't seen it at all.

Downstairs, he heard movement. The sound of voices and a door opening. Footsteps in the hall. He lifted his creation slowly; his breath seemed to be stuck in his throat. He couldn't drop it, not again. She had to see this one, and she would like it much more. It would make her smile. He moved on to the landing and heard them talking in the hall, the tops of their heads showing over the top of the bannister. Granddad's shiny bald patch, Dad's dark curls. She was by the stairs, looking up. Looking right up at him.

"I made this for you," he said, holding it up high so she could see it. He wanted to see her eyes light up. He wanted her to come upstairs and really look at it. He wanted to touch her and have her close to him again.

But Dad took her hand and she looked away.

"I made this for you!" he said, louder.

Dad's eyes were wide and sad. "We have to go," he said. "We can't be late. We can look at your spaceship when we get back."

It wasn't a spaceship, stupid man. It was a house.

He watched them walk away. She didn't look at him again. He wanted her too, but she didn't want him.

A blink and they were gone.

She was gone again.

The Lego house tumbled to the ground, its tiny pieces falling into the space where she had stood.

Chapter Three

I always walk back home past the beach now. I kind of have to. It's like I need to be there as much as possible because it's the only connection I have left. It was something that had been ours.

One day I stop by the lightning tree, looking up. This old tree always seems to call me back. When I was little, it had seemed so *big* – scary even. But now it's frail-looking, the way its bark splinters like a rotten fingernail jabbing into the blue sky. I almost felt sorry for it, this dead thing that has been left here to stand for the rest of time.

"Are you going to start talking to *that* too?"

Oh God. Not again.

I rolled my eyes, not even needing to turn around to know who it was. That girl again.

I carried on walking.

"Really friendly, aren't you?" she said, walking behind me, her tone light. Mocking, maybe.

This was getting a bit annoying now.

"Are you following me or something?" I shot back.

She laughed. One of those "ooh, get you" kind of laughs, high and irritating. "No! Why would I do that?"

I stopped. "You just seem to be everywhere I am."

She held her hands up in mock defence "Look, I don't know what your problem is. But I'm not following you, OK? This is my way home." She sniffed. "I'm not that tragic."

I paused, a prickle of unease passing through me. "Look – I'm sorry. I didn't mean that. I just. . ." I sighed. "I just like being on my own at the moment."

She snorted. "I worked that out."

"It's nothing to do with you. . . I dunno. . ." I shifted on the spot. "I'm not good around people right now."

She half nodded. "Fair enough. I get that. And look, I didn't mean to wind you up the other day by the beach. I was only joking. I'm sorry."

I paused, and the words hung between us. In front of me, amongst the bushes to the side, deep within the leaves, a small wren peered back at me. I've always liked wrens. I kept still, not wanting to disturb it.

"I was talking to a bird," I said finally.

"Oh. OK."

She was standing a little way behind me, her thin arms wrapped round her body as if she was cold, a large bag hanging from her shoulder, seeming to pull down one entire half of her. Her long hair was tangled around her face, where a small smile played on her lips.

"Talking to birds is weird, is it?" I asked her accusingly.

"No. Not at all."

"Then what's so funny?"

"You! You're just so ... I dunno, uptight!" Her smile spread. "This is no big deal, but you're stomping around like I peed on your sandwiches or something."

I couldn't help grinning back. "Well, to be fair, peeing on my sandwiches *would* be a step too far."

She walked towards me. "I promise I won't. I have fantastic bladder control anyway."

"That's good to know."

"Anyway, like I said, I'm sorry. I was out of order before. Sometimes I speak before thinking."

She paused, her large eyes staring at mine.

"But to be honest, we've just moved here and it'd be nice to talk to someone. I mean, I live with a load of little kids. It does my head in. I need to get outside. I need to get away from them, you know?"

I sighed. People. Talk. It was the last thing I wanted. And I was about to say so when she shivered and pulled her arms tighter around herself.

"I don't know anyone here. It's been a tough move," she said.

I hesitated. "Where did you live before?"

"South London. We had to move quickly. Things got ... tricky." Her head dropped, and her dark hair seemed to spill everywhere.

"Look, I'm not sure—"

She jerked her head up again, her eyes bright and intent. "I was just interested in what you were doing the other morning. Up so early. I don't know anyone else who gets up at that time. I thought I was the only one."

I shifted on the spot. "Well... It's a good time to be out. I like it when it's quiet."

And I also don't sleep much these days. I lie awake for hours most nights. And others, well, others I wake up and can't get back off.

But you don't need to know that about me.

"I get that. I like it quiet too."

I sighed. "Look—"

I stopped short as I realized I didn't even know her name.

"Alice," she said softly.

"Look, Alice. It's nice meeting you and everything and I really hope that you like it here. But I've got a lot of stuff on at the moment, do you know what I mean?"

And I don't want anyone new in my life, OK?

She nodded. "Yeah. I know what you mean."

"I hope . . . well, it was nice meeting you," I said stiffly.

God, that didn't sound like me at all. Not like the old me, anyway. It sounded like something my dad would say to a stranger he'd met at the pub.

"You too. . ."

She looked at me wide-eyed. Her smile was back. I liked her smile, actually. It was warm and bright. Real.

"Alfie," I told her.

"You too, *Alfie*."

I kicked at the pavement. "So are you going back to your new house?"

For a moment I swore I saw a shiver of something pass across her face. But then she just smiled again and shrugged. "Nah, I might stay here for a bit, go back over to the beach. I like it there." I can't say I blamed her. I like it there too.

I half waved, which made me feel a bit stupid. Then I turned and went. I should have felt good. I should've felt relieved. I'd wanted to go, after all. But something else pulled at me, something heavier... Guilt, I guess. She was new. She was lonely. I should have stayed and been friendly.

I should've done the right thing.

I turned back.

I watched her as she moved towards the beach before stopping at the bench at the end of the field, the one that faced the sea. She sat down slowly, lowering her bag beside her, her eyes cast out towards the water. She looked really still.

And alone.

I wanted to go back. That was the right thing to do. The old Alfie would've done that for sure. I would've sat right down next to her and had a full-on conversation. I would've asked about her life, told her all the gossip from school.

But this Alfie is tired. This Alfie has no room for other people, or their problems.

So this Alfie headed home and tried not to think about her.

It had been two days. Two days and she had not come downstairs at all.

He stood at the bottom step and looked up. He could just about see her closed door. The light at the bottom a soft, enticing glow. He longed to creep up, push open the door and crawl into her bed like he used to.

"Mum? Mum! Are you OK? Can I come up?"

He went up a few steps, a nervous feeling creeping into his tummy, like icy fingers tickling his insides. He looked up at the door again. Why was he frightened? He's always been brave. Everyone said so.

"...Mum?"

He took another step. He needed to see her. It had been too long.

But he felt a shadow behind him, and a large hand gripped his shoulder.

Dad.

"No, Alfie, come away. She needs to rest."

He only wanted to talk to her. Tell her that the robin had come back. She wouldn't see from her front window. She needed to be at the back. She needed to look into the trees.

"Come on." Dad was gently tugging on his arm. But he didn't want to move. He shook off his Dad and moved upwards again. Nearer to the closed door. The scary closed door.

Nearer to her.

He could hear noises up there. Horrible gagging noises. It sounded awful, like she was choking. Not like her at all. More like an animal.

He spun around and looked up at his dad, hoping to see something that would reassure him. Make him feel better. Maybe he would tell him what was going on. And then it would be OK. Everything would be OK.

But his dad was staring up at the closed door too, his face frozen in sadness. His other hand was bunched up against his mouth. His eyes were squeezed shut.

He was crying.

Chapter Four

The door was unlocked when I got home, which meant he was back early. I hesitated in surprise before putting my keys away. Dad had been doing quite a good job of staying late at work recently, and we both knew that it was on purpose.

I walked in and threw my bag down in the hall. I heard him straight away. He was playing his music in the kitchen – some rubbish eighties band that he desperately tried to make me like. I glanced at the stairs, wondering if I could head straight to my room and avoid him altogether. But that seemed a step too far. So instead I made my way towards the kitchen.

He was cooking. To be fair, Dad is a decent cook, when he can be bothered, and when I saw the curry bubbling away my stomach growled instinctively. He turned around, wooden spoon clutched in his hand.

"All right, son? I was starving and thought I'd knock up something decent for a change."

I nodded. It certainly *was* a change. Most of the time it was either takeouts or beans on toast.

Dad is a big guy, who always seems to take over any room he is in. And by *big* I don't mean that he's fat – he's muscular. He used to work out – years ago, before all this happened – and now he's kind of square and stocky, with huge meaty arms and a head that seems to sit solidly on his massive chest. My mates always used to be scared of him, thinking he was some kind of gangster or thug. I guess I used to find that funny. But the truth is that he's not a scary guy at all. He's just a bloke that works in a warehouse and drinks down the local pub. I don't think he's ever even been in a fight. He stays out of trouble. He's quiet like that.

"How was your day?" he asked, giving his curry another stir.

"Not bad."

I sat down and pulled his newspaper over the table so I could pretend to read the sports page that he'd left open, even though I didn't give a toss. I glanced at the title. This wasn't his usual paper.

"West Ham lost again," he said.

"Yeah..." I wasn't reading that. I was looking at the crossword. It looked familiar. Wasn't this the one Mum used to spend hours doing? Yeah... This was the paper she usually picked, not Dad. Wasn't that the only reason she bought this paper? For the crossword? Half the time she'd never finish it and would get all frustrated and throw it in the bin.

"Is this the paper Mum used to buy?" I asked, pointing at it.

Dad turned to me, a small scowl on his face. "What? No... I can't remember. It was the last one in the shop. I only got it to read about the game, which, seriously, was a shocker. The manager needs to be sacked."

No. No... I don't want to hear about the game, Dad. I want to hear about Mum.

"This *is* the same one. I'm sure... She always did this crossword, remember? She liked it."

Dad shrugged with his back to me. "Maybe. It was the only paper left."

"She loved her puzzles."

"Alfie..."

He turned, and I saw that his face was stretched into some weird smile. He wiped his hand across his mouth, like he'd been sweating. "Alfie. You didn't tell me about your day. Did you go to football?"

"I don't do football any more. I told you."

He shook his head. "I just thought you might have changed your mind."

"Well, I haven't. I'm not going to either."

He looked at me like I was some kind of alien. Like he really couldn't work me out. Then he shook his head and went back to the dinner.

"This'll be ready in half an hour," he muttered.

I took my cue to leave.

My room is still full of football trophies, medals, photos – the lot. I guess you could say I used to be quite a good player. Maybe I could even make it as a pro. I had been playing since the age of six. I started out just having fun with my mates and ended up being one of the best midfielders in our county.

But not any more, I just can't face it. It will never feel the same for me. And nobody ever seems to understand why. On my desk sits my largest award – manager's player of the year. A great big shiny thing, given to me in June a year ago.

Just a year ago.

I remember the awards evening. I had been twelve and I hadn't even wanted to go. I told them all that I didn't want to be there, but they insisted. They said it was important. Someone – was it Dad? – said it might even help me.

Help me? Like that could help. They honestly didn't have a clue. None of them did.

Dad came, of course. He had to, I guess. He said he wanted to be there, but I remember us driving to clubhouse in silence. I even sat in the back – I couldn't stand to sit in the front because that's where she should've been. I stared at the back of that empty seat all the way there. Dad didn't chat like he usually did. He didn't even put on the radio. There was just this cloud of unsaid words hanging between us, words that were so obvious the silence was almost deafening.

She's not here.

She's gone.

It's different now.

This is for ever.

It's just us now.

The entire Cookbridge team was at the clubhouse. Rhys, Charlie, Cole from school. . . Cole had looked at me like I was a stranger. I dunno, maybe I felt that way too. And that was the start of it – the start of everyone treating me differently. I sat with them, at the same table, I listened to them talking and joking, but they could barely bring themselves to look at me, except for when they flashed me sympathetic smiles like I was some kind of loser. It felt like they were afraid of me. It was like I was carrying some silent disease that they were scared of catching. I remember gripping the side of the table, watching as the tips of my fingers turned white, praying that it would all be over quickly.

It's all right lads. I won't show you up by crying.

I'll just pretend, OK?

I'll just pretend everything is the same as always.

I'm getting good at pretending. Look. . .

When Rob the manager called my name up, I barely heard him. There was loads of clapping, whistling too, but I couldn't move. It was as if I was stuck to my seat. I looked back at my dad, who was sitting with the other parents. He was smiling back at me but his smile looked forced. On the seat next to him was some bloke with mad frizzy hair. Why was *he* sitting there? It should've been her. She loved going to things like this. She'd always been proud, always encouraged me. And now ... now *what*? I was being cheered on by my exhausted dad and a load of strangers with wide, strained smiles.

I couldn't do it. I couldn't move.

Cole glared at me. "They're waiting for you," he whispered. Cole didn't like the team being shown up and I could tell he was getting annoyed with me. So I staggered up there – took the longest walk ever to the front of the room, with all those eyes on me, all of them staring, while my stomach was flipping over. I wanted to puke. At the front, Rob took my arm. He was a cool bloke. He knew what had been going on. He looked down at me and smiled sadly.

"You OK, son?"

I nodded.

He squeezed my shoulder and then turned back to the room. "It gives me great pleasure to present this award to Alfie Turner today. Not only is he one of the most gifted midfielders I have seen in a long time, but he is a true professional. I know he has had interest from a few – well, shall we say *very large* clubs. The future looks very bright for this young man..."

The future looks bright...

The words buzzed in my brain. Bright? How could it possibly be bright? The trophy was placed in my hand, but I wasn't paying attention. I was looking again.

Looking for my mum in the audience. I needed her. I needed her to see this.

How couldn't she be here?

It was all wrong.

They wanted me to say something. They wanted me to say thanks, to have some well-prepared speech. I opened my mouth and nothing came out. I had nothing. Except, I realized, as I searched for her face in the crowd, tears. Yeah, that's right, tears. Loads of them.

I stood there and sobbed like a baby in front of the entire county football team and their parents while I looked for a mum who was no longer there.

She had been dead for precisely three weeks.

She sat him down next to her. It was a warm spring morning and they were squeezed together on the swing seat. This was one of her favourite places to be, under the shade but in full view of the trees. You could see the entire garden from here.

She didn't talk to begin with; she just gently rocked them both. It was so soothing that he thought he might fall asleep.

"Alfie, I'm very poorly," she said. "I have been for a while."

Her words seemed to catch on the breeze and fly away. He couldn't quite hear them. He looked up at her, confused. Not just poorly. Very poorly. What did that mean?

"I'm very poorly," she said again, taking his hand in hers. "I found a lump ages ago and the doctors took it away. But now I have another one."

41

"What does that mean?"

She seemed to think about this for a moment before answering him. "It's cancer, Alfie. And it's more aggressive this time, which means it's harder to make it go away. The only way doctors can get rid of the tumour is by giving me medicine and then zapping it with radiation."

He nodded. That did make sense. "Is that what's making you sick?"

"Yes. And I'm going to be very tired a lot of the time, because my body needs to work on making me better. That's quite a hard job and it wears me out."

"Like after I've run a lot at football?"

She laughed. "Yes. Yes, just like that. That's a bit like how Mum feels right now."

"Dad said you will sleep a lot."

She nodded. Her eyes looked odd, so big and glassy. "And I won't be able to come and see you play football, Alfie. Not at the moment. I need to rest. I can't go out too much in case I catch any bugs – do you understand?"

"Like a cold?"

"Yes. When I have my next treatment I'm going to stay in hospital because my body will be very weak. You and Dad need to look after each other here until I'm a bit stronger. Is that OK?"

He didn't like how this was making him feel. "Will you be OK, Mum?"

She was still rocking them slowly.

Back and forth.

Back and forth.

He didn't like the silence. It scared him.

"I'm not going to lie to you, Alfie. This is a serious thing. But the doctors are doing all they can treat it and I feel positive that it will be OK."

He snuggled in close to her. She felt so small, but so safe. "I don't want you to be ill."

"Neither do I, Alfie. Hopefully I'll be better really soon."

That was the day when he knew everything was going to change.

He was nine years old

Chapter Five

I didn't leave the house as early this time, mainly because the lack of sleep was catching up with me, making it that little bit harder to drag myself out of bed. But I still managed to get up before seven, which was something.

I didn't want to be in the house on my own.

I'm still not used to this. She'd always been here, unless she was having treatment. Even if she was in bed, she'd still be here, and it was good just knowing that. Hearing her music playing. Seeing her books lying around. Having parts of her here with me. But now it's just us. Me and Dad. Or, most of the time, just me. Me and my old memories rattling around in my head. Every part of her is packed away now, Dad has made sure of that. He can't bear to have her stuff around, reminding us, so there is nothing of her here now. No books, no clothes...

Nothing.

I remember the day he did that – packed everything away. He had boxes everywhere and great big bin bags strewn across the room. It was like he saw her stuff as rubbish. Things to be thrown away.

"She wanted her clothes to go to charity," he told me, not even looking at me as he stuffed more of them into the bag.

"Already?"

I was standing there, watching him, not able to move. She'd barely been gone and he was doing this already.

"I need to," he said.

I didn't understand him. It was like he wanted to forget. Did he not think I'd noticed that their wedding photo had disappeared from the living room too? What had he done with *that*? Shoved it in the charity bag with one of her old T-shirts? Chucked it into the bin?

"It's *too soon*. This is her stuff."

"It's just clothes. We don't need them."

Just clothes. I remember thinking how cold his voice sounded.

I watched as he rammed a dress in next. It was the pretty blue-and-white one, one of mum's favourites. Now it was getting all crumpled.

"Be careful – you're ruining it."

He ignored me, threw the bag on the bed and started to gather up more of her belongings in his huge, useless arms.

"You don't even care, do you?" I shouted.

No reply. His arms kept on working, faster now, shoving more of her things away. It felt cruel.

I hated him.

"You wanted this."

He turned, his eyes blazing back at me. "What? *What* did I want?"

I leant in, and could feel each word as it spat from my lips. "You wanted her dead. You're just sorry it took so long."

He froze then, still gripping the bag in his hands. Then he let it go, dropping it down by his feet, spilling out the contents. He looked at me, his eyes blazing, and his mouth was moving but nothing was coming out. I knew he wanted to say something, and I stepped back, waiting for his words to hit me. I wanted them to.

But he simply shook his head and walked past me out of the room.

The next day everything of Mum's was gone. There was nothing left at all.

And Dad didn't speak to me for a week.

I was quick in the shower and dressed at speed. They both used to laugh at the crazy amount of time I spent in the bathroom doing my hair, making myself look good. Now that all seems pointless. I flattened it down with the palm of my hand and brushed my teeth, barely even glancing at myself in the mirror.

I didn't have breakfast. The lead ball that sat in my stomach made me feel full up. And as I walked down the path, I half wondered if I'd see her again. *Alice*. I also wondered why I suddenly cared. She was definitely unusual. A lot different from the other girls at school, with her wild hair and confident attitude. I guess there was something about her that intrigued me. As I got closer to the field, it was clear she wasn't there, not yet anyway, so I crossed over the grass as usual and walked to the seafront. It was still pretty quiet. A few gulls were on the water, and right over on the other side of the beach a raven was picking at a sticking out piece of bark. I watched it for a bit.

Ravens are pretty cool. When I'd see one as a kid, I'd convince myself that it was the same one that came back time and time again. Like it was a guardian of the beach or something.

I didn't stay long. I couldn't get comfortable, and all I could think of was the cold creeping through my coat and into my bones, making it difficult to concentrate.

I got up slowly.

"Leaving already?"

Alice was standing on the other side of me, leaning up against the railings. Her arms were wrapped tightly around her body, the wind whipping her hair around, making it look more wild than ever. At least this time she was wearing a coat, even though it was a pretty thin denim one. Her legs were bare – she must have been really cold. She was still carrying that huge bag of hers.

I shrugged. "I guess I'm not in the mood."

"Bit early for school?"

I glanced at my watch. It was quarter to eight.

"I walk the long way round."

"Can I join you?"

I considered her for a minute. I usually went the longer way to avoid Cole and the others. The people

I used to walk to school with. But what was I meant to say? *"No, go away. I'd rather be on my own."* I didn't want to be rude to her again.

I shrugged instead.

"You really don't talk much, do you?" she said as we started walking along the road.

"Not really."

She snorted. "It's like talking to a brick."

"Thanks." I looked over at her, really not sure how to take that, but she was grinning, her long hair falling into her face. She kept pushing it back, fighting with the wind.

"So, where does this longer route take us?"

"We have to cut through the field again, go past the park and then across the housing estate. It's about twenty minutes longer."

"OK, well I know the park. That's kind of where I'm living now."

"The park?" I said, obviously confused.

"Oh sure! I've got a sleeping bag under the slide!" She nudged me. "Are you for real? We're staying in one of the houses near it. On Bourne Road."

That was a decent road. It ran off one of the posher streets. All the houses there were dead nice.

"Wow. Those places are huge."

"Aren't they just?" Her smile widened. "You sound surprised."

"No, I just. . ." I found myself stammering. "I didn't think. . ."

"You didn't think I looked posh enough to live there."

"It's not that!"

"You think I look poor or something?"

She had stopped now and was standing with her hands on her hips, staring at me. I looked at her thin coat, her thin face, her messy hair. Did I think that?

I shook my head. "I don't know what I thought."

"Well, you don't know anything," she said.

We carried on walking in silence.

But now all I wanted her to do was talk.

He went into her room one morning and watched as she did her hair. It had always been long, thick and curly. She usually complained about it – about the knots and how much time it took to do anything with it. But now she was silent. Her hands ran through the strands slowly.

He watched as her fingers came away, long blonde curls twisted around them like golden twine.

"It's going," she said softly. "It's all going."

"Mum..."

He didn't know what to say. She looked so sad. Too sad. He hated seeing her like this.

"I'm like a tree losing its leaves for winter," she said, her eyes still fixed on the mirror. "Soon it'll all be bare. And what will be left of me?"

"You'll have no hair?"

She looked over him then, like she had finally noticed

him in the room. A tiny smile crept across her face. "It's OK, Alfie, it'll grow back. It's only hair. There's more important things."

But it was her hair. Her beautiful hair. She was changing.

Breaking...

"I don't want you to lose it."

"Neither do I. But I am."

He thought about this for a bit. "Lots of footballers have shaved heads. They look cool."

She smiled. "That's true. Would you think I was cool if I shaved my head?"

He grinned and nodded.

"Maybe I'll get a wig though, for when I go outside," she said, almost to herself, still looking in the mirror. "A fantastic one. You can help me chose it."

"Really?"

She beamed. "Why not? It'll be fun."

Later that day, he marched up to his dad.

"I want you to shave my head."

His dad stared down at him, a confused look passing across his face.

"What?"

"I don't want mum to be the only one. I want to be like her."

His dad paused for a second. "Fair enough," he said.

They went into the kitchen and he sat down on the high bar stool while his dad put newspaper on the floor to catch the hair. The vibration felt oddly soothing against his skin; the buzzing noise was comforting. He watched as his spiky blonde hair fell to the floor in tiny golden shards.

His dad stopped. "There!" he said, running a hand over his head. "It actually looks good."

"Really?"

"Really."

Then Alfie watched as his dad turned round and, using the tiny mirror on the kitchen window sill, put the clippers against his own thick hair.

"We can all be the same," he announced, running the blade across his head. "We can all do this together."

Chapter Six

Ben grabbed me outside of tutor group.

"Where were you this morning? I was actually ready early today. I waited for you."

I looked up at him and almost staggered back in shock. "Seriously, mate, how are you getting away with that?"

His hair was even brighter today, and he'd spiked it into a more obvious Mohican style. Plus, he was wearing bright blue eyeliner.

Ben grinned. "I told you, Malone has his own issues right now. He barely notices any of us."

"Yeah, but the other teachers. Are they blind or something?" I shook my head in disbelief and we both started walking to class.

"It's my charm – they can't see beyond it."

"I swear you're just looking for attention."

"Maybe." Ben shifted his bag on to his other arm. "Anything to brighten an otherwise dull day. Anyway, where were you this morning?"

I frowned at him. "I walked the other way. But you can't have a go at me about that. You're never normally ready."

"Fair enough. I was more interested in the girl you walked in with."

I could feel my entire body cringe. I hoped my cheeks weren't flushing bright red. "Since when have you started spying on me?"

He snorted. "Hardly spying. I just happened to be in school early and I saw you both. I have to say, I was a little surprised. . ."

I didn't want to take the bait, but he triggered something in me. "What do you mean?"

"Well . . . she doesn't seem your normal type."

My normal type! What the hell did Ben know anyway? No one knew my "normal type".

Not even me. . .

"Stop that!" I snapped. "I was just walking in with her, nothing else. I felt sorry for her. She's new. She doesn't know anyone."

"Aw! You were doing a good deed. . ."

"Yeah. And?"

Ben stopped walking and held his hands up in mock defeat. "And, good! I'm pleased. You don't need to get so wound up. It's cool that you did a nice thing."

"Yeah – well stop going on about her," I muttered. "It's not like that. I don't fancy her. I don't even like her. She's actually really annoying."

Ben nodded. "Fair enough."

I stared back at him, suddenly curious. "Hang on a minute. Why were you in school so early? You wouldn't be on time even if you were paid to."

Ben smiled. "Oh, didn't I tell you? I've joined the drama group. I'm helping design the set for the next A-level piece. Thought I'd come in early to help."

I looked at him confused. "So. . ."

"So. . . Becky Collins is in charge of set design."

I got through most of the day OK. It actually wasn't that bad, and at least I could keep myself amused thinking about Ben and his latest obsession. This wasn't a new thing for Ben. Last term he'd been in love with Olivia Graham in year eleven, which lasted all of six weeks until he found out she supported fox hunting and then suddenly realized she wasn't so cool. I guess I quite like the way that Ben is so over-the-top and dramatic. It's a good distraction. Plus, he's never weird around me, he just acts like he always has, and I appreciate that. It makes a difference.

I've known Ben since primary school. We were actually really good friends in the first two years, inventing crazy playground games and freaking out the girls with stupid dares and tricks. He always made me laugh and we'd get into trouble for messing around. Mum loved him though. She said he was a "star in the making" and that he would end up on stage.

And Ben liked Mum. He was always dead polite, would call her Mrs Franks, and blush whenever she complimented him. He used to tell me I was lucky having a mum like her, someone who was so relaxed about rules and who was pretty chilled-out most of the time. I don't think it was like that for Ben. I think he and his mum argued a lot. In fact, they still do.

We drifted apart when I got into football, because Ben wasn't into sport. He always said his brain was wired differently and it meant that he couldn't throw, catch or run in a straight line. He was forever bringing in sick notes to skip PE and sit in the library instead. But I loved football. And I was good at it. By year three I was in the town's best football team and by year four, my new best mate was Cole Stephens, the good striker with a big gob.

Ben started to hang around with other kids, people I didn't really know, and I guess we both moved on.

That was until a month after mum died. I was sitting alone in the lunch hall at school – which was my choice. I could've sat with Cole and the others, but I didn't want to. I wasn't in the mood to listen to their banter, to pretend to be OK and laugh along with the rest of them. Cole didn't want me to talk about my mum. None of them did. I just made them feel uncomfortable

But then Ben suddenly appeared next to me.

"All right, loser?"

I remember how I'd looked up at his familiar, friendly face and felt a wave of something. I think it was relief.

"It's awful about your mum. You must really miss her."

"Yeah."

He didn't seem to be bothered by my stupid teary eyes or the fact that I was sniffing back snot. He just said, "Well, I'm here for you mate," and sat down next to me.

Last period of the day was PE, which I was kind of dreading. How ironic that what used to be my best subject has ended up being my worst. And how tragic that my so-called teammate and old best friend has ended up being the person I most dread being with.

As soon as I walked into the changing rooms, Cole was there, in the middle of everyone, loud and lairy as normal. He turned as I walked in. "Alfie! Mate. You missed my latest update."

I stared back at him, trying to look unimpressed. I knew it was going to be some stupid boast of his. He always has to be the centre of attention.

"What's up?"

"I was spotted by a scout," he said, full-on grinning at me. "At last week's game. He's going to recommend me for a trial, thinks I could be academy level."

"Really?" I nodded, throwing my bag on the bench. "That's great news."

Mr Rogers walked in then, slamming the door behind him as usual. "Boys, boys! What's with all this standing around? You should be ready by now."

Riley, one of Cole's biggest suck-ups, piped up.

"Cole was telling us his news, sir. He's been scouted – might be playing for a professional club soon."

"Really?" Mr Rogers' eyebrow raised, and I saw him flick a quick glance to me. "That's great, Cole, well done. But let's not get carried away – you're not Messi yet and you've still got a dodgeball game to play."

Cole sniggered. I felt him give me another look, but I busied myself getting ready as everyone filtered out of the room.

Mr Rogers was still standing there, though.

"Have you had trials recently, Alfie?" he said.

"No," I said firmly. "I'm not doing football at the moment."

"I get that, lad. You need time and that." He sighed. "But if you do ever change your mind, I still know people. You're such a talent, it'd be a shame to waste it."

I pulled on my PE top. "I'm just not interested any more."

"Funny that," Mr Rogers said, turning to walk away. "I could have sworn that when Cole was announcing his news right then, you looked sick with jealously. . ."

I opened my mouth to protest but he'd already walked off.

He came back covered in mud. It had been one of those games where he'd spent most of the match skidding about on the grass. But what a match! Dad had slapped his back afterwards, beaming with pride.

"You made a fool of the lot of them out there, Alfie. You were amazing."

They walked home. He was so stiff with mud, he could barely move, but he didn't care. The sun had come out and it was warm on his skin. He felt like he was ten inches taller.

They walked around the side gate, so as not to traipse mud into the house. He was surprised to see her outside already, digging away at the soft earth at the back of the garden.

He ran over to her.

"We won six-two. I scored a hat trick and set two of the other goals up!"

She swept him up in a hug, not caring how mucky he was. He squeezed her back tight. She still felt small and bony, but her grip was strong. When she let go of him she was still smiling. Her face seemed brighter today, but he noticed that she was wearing a bit of make-up. Her blonde hair was starting to grow back in small curls. He wished that she could come watch him play, but at least she was here. And she was smiling. Really smiling.

"I'm so proud of you – you're such a superstar," she said.

Dad came over. "His coach says he's getting stronger by the day."

She grinned. "He's not the only one."

They looked over at the patch of soil she'd been digging. There was a scattering of golden seed in the dark earth.

"Sunflowers," she said. "I'm planting them here, by the fence, so that they can catch the sunlight and grow really tall."

He felt excited. "I love sunflowers."

His mum squeezed his hand. "So do I. And we can watch them grow. As we get better and better, they will grow taller and taller."

He looked down at the brown soil, at the tiny holes she had made. A heavy feeling drifted down into his stomach, and he had to quickly look away again, before the feeling shifted. Before he was sick.

Because what if they didn't grow at all? What if they never grew tall?

What if she never got better?

Chapter Seven

I found myself back at the seafront, sea whipping my hair, tears stinging my cheeks. If the sea had been louder I would have shouted some words into it. Everything seemed so unfair, everything. I felt like the waves – rough, out of control, raging.

How can I ever play again? How could it ever be the same again?

Why did this have to happen to me?

She shouldn't have died. It wasn't right. None of this was right...

I gripped the railings. I realized I was shaking, and blinked back my tears. I would not let myself break down. Not here. Not ever.

I had to hold it together.

I had gone home before, but Dad wasn't there again and I couldn't handle the empty house. He'd left me some money – a tenner – so I could get myself a pizza or a ready meal, or something. Anything so he didn't have to think too much about me.

I pulled out the ten-pound note and held it in my hand. I was so tempted to just rip it up and throw the pieces into the wind. After all, he wouldn't care, would he? He barely knew what I was up to one day from the next.

"What are you doing?"

I spun around, feeling angry at being caught by surprise.

"Are you following me?" I snapped.

Alice raised her hands up in mock defence. "Chill! Seriously! I told you before. I'm not following you. I only live over there, remember." She sighed. "I came out to buy some chips and I saw you standing there looking like you're about to throw your money away."

I stuffed the note back in my pocket. "I wasn't."

"If you don't want it. . ." Her eyes were sparkling.

"Of course I do. I was only messing around."

"Well, I'm going to get some chips. Fancy some?" She grinned. "Chips always cheer me up."

I really didn't and was about to say no, but then I

thought of my empty house. Of Dad's usual scrawled note left for me. I couldn't face going back yet. What else was there for me to do?

So I shrugged. "OK."

Alice stuffed a chip in her mouth and licked her salty finger.

"I've got more interesting ways of spending that tenner," she said, daring me to challenge her. Daring me to ask her more. I said nothing, just ate the few remaining chips I had left. I'd been surprised by how hungry I actually was once I could smell that salt and vinegar smell. We were walking away from the seafront now and towards the high street, well away from the seagulls that would've only tried to steal our food.

"Aren't you interested?" she asked, tipping the rest of the packet into her mouth to catch the tiny flecks of batter that were left behind.

"I haven't got a tenner now, have I?" I muttered, stuffing my rubbish in the nearby bin. "You just made me buy you chips."

"*Made you*?" Her eyes glinted. "Oh yeah, of course, I *made* you walk over to that van and order it."

"I wasn't that bothered. It was only because you

wanted them. And anyway, it's lucky I did buy them, otherwise you'd still be starving."

She shrugged. "I forgot my wallet. It happens. I'll pay you back if it's such a big deal."

"It's OK, it doesn't matter. But I've not got a tenner now, that's all."

Alice nudged me and pointed. "You see that shop on the corner, the newsagent? They're dead soft in there. You could grab us some chocolate and they wouldn't even bat an eye."

I stared back at her. "What, steal it?" Was she being serious?

"Yeah, *steal*," she giggled. "Just a couple of small bars. It'll be a nice treat. They won't even care."

I stopped walking, and looked over at the tatty newsagent over the road. I'd been there before, of course. Bought chewing gum, stuff like that. It was run by some guy who spent the majority of the time watching the TV by his till. I knew its reputation – some of the kids in my year said you could buy stuff there even if you were underage. I never bothered with all that though. Smoking, drinking ... none of that had ever appealed to me, because I had to be so careful about what I put into my body – that mattered if I wanted to do well in football. I had to show discipline too and keep myself out of trouble. I didn't do things like this normally, nothing illegal anyway.

But I'm not that person now.

"Why should I have to do it?" I said finally. "It's your idea."

"You're older. And anyway, I've challenged you," Alice replied simply. "I'll wait on that bench over there," she said, pointing loosely to one by the bandstand. "Go on – it won't take long. I really fancy something sweet."

So… She really did want me to do? But what did I have to lose?

I strolled over to the shop, trying to act casual. This was no big deal. I was going to grab some chocolate bars and go. As I pushed open the heavy wooden door I tried to keep calm. No one would suspect I was planning anything. I just needed to act cool.

This was no big deal.

The sweets and chocolates were all lined up at the back so I made my way down the aisle, avoiding a tiny elderly woman who was loading up a basket at the front shelves. I needed to be confident here. My eyes flicked up to the small CCTV camera in the corner of the ceiling. It was pointing my way but looked blank. Was it even on?

Quickly, I snatched a couple of bars and slid them into my pocket. They feel heavy and bulky sitting there, but I tried to ignore them. I tried to act casual.

There you go, Alice, it's easy.

The shop owner was glued to the TV screen as I approached him. He was middle-aged and tired looking, and he barely looked up when I walked up to the counter. Quickly, I reached up and selected some chewing gum. It wasn't even the flavour I liked. I passed the packet over to him.

He nodded lazily and ran it through the till, not even bothering to speak. Not even looking at me properly. Perhaps if he did he would've seen the bulge in my pocket, or the guilty glow in my cheeks.

I laid my money on the counter, thanked him and quickly walked out. My heart was pounding and I literally felt like I would puke as soon as I pushed open the door. Surely he knew what I had done?

Would he chase me out? Shout something?

Would his hand grab my collar?

But there was nothing. As I stepped back out into the cool air, I knew I had got away with it. I couldn't believe how much my heart was beating inside my chest and how icy my stomach felt.

Alice was waiting a little way down the street, a tiny smirk etched on her face.

"You did it, then?"

I rammed the bars into her hand. And the stupid chewing gum. "I don't even want them," I said. "And I'm not doing that again."

"Calm down," she giggled. "It's only a bit of fun."

Strange that it didn't feel that way to me.

We went back on the seafront and sat on the beach. It was still cold but I was beyond caring. Alice had eaten both the chocolate bars and the wrappers lay at her feet.

"I still can't believe you did that," I said. "Are you really hungry or something?"

"Yeah, I guess. Didn't get a chance to eat much at home earlier."

I stretched out, liking the feeling of the stones shifting beneath me.

"You should've seen your face when you came out of there. You looked like you'd seen a ghost," she said, nudging me.

"I thought I was going to collapse. That was really stressful."

"You're so funny!" She smiled up at me. "You're such a Mr Stress-Head."

"I just worry – that's all." I frowned. "I don't usually do stuff like that."

It was getting dark but I didn't care. I closed my eyes and breathed in the salty, cool air.

"Your phone is buzzing again," Alice said, nodding towards my mobile. I glanced at the screen and cringed.

"It's no one. He can wait."

I thought of Dad at home, wondering where I was. I was surprised he'd even noticed. The thought of it made me laugh. Maybe he'd actually remembered that he had a son.

"I told you this was a good idea," Alice said.

I nodded. "Yeah. It was."

I was chilled. I was calm.

I wasn't thinking.

It was all good for once.

His dad took his hand before the game started.

"This is your chance. This is your chance to show them what you're made of. Do well today and you could be selected for the team."

He nodded, feeling a little sick but excited too. Across the pitch he could see Cole warming up with the rest of the team. He already knew Cole was good; he was forever boasting at school.

His dad gave him a gentle nudge. "Go on. They're waiting for you."

He jogged over, his tummy tight, his blood pumping. This was a big deal. Cookbridge United was the best team in the county. And now this was his opportunity to show them that he belonged with them. The words of his old coach rattled in his head: "You deserve this, mate. You're good enough."

The boys looked up as he approached. They seemed

older than him, even though he knew they were under eights too. A couple of them smiled but one or two scowled. Cole just stared, looking cool.

"You came then?"

"Yeah, your coach said I could give it a go."

Rob strolled over. He was a big guy with a huge head of messy dark curls. He beamed down at him.

"Alfie? You came! Nice one. I'm looking forward to seeing you train. You can show us what you're made of."

"Not a lot, probably," said Cole, but he had a smile on his face.

They started with basic warm ups and a few passing exercises – stuff he was used to. He kept his head down, knowing the other kids were eying him up. He was a potential rival, after all, someone who could steal their spot.

Rob blew his whistle and told them they were going to play a match.

"I hear you're a midfielder. Wanna go left wing?"

He nodded.

Cole was still staring at him. He was in the other team. A striker, of course, eyes gleaming. Alert.

The whistle blew again.

His side were moving forward, advancing fast, but no one was passing to him. He was open, shouting for the ball. But he didn't know names yet. He didn't know who to call for. The ball was being kicked everywhere, but it was nowhere near him.

Cole scooted past him. "Aw, never mind. Maybe you're not up to it?"

He shook him off and ran down the wing to his own half. The other team had the ball, but he moved in, sliding a brilliant tackle through and winning it back.

He turned. The ball was his now.

So he ran. Fast.

They came at him. One clumsy tackle from behind, one shoulder charge at his side, but he skipped past them easily. The last defender approached from the penalty area, ready to slide in, but that wasn't going to happen. Alfie saw the tackle and cut inside with the ball, leaving the defender on the floor. He opened up his body, ready to place the shot behind the advancing keeper, and slugged the ball – hard but controlled.

He could hear his dad's cheer from the other side of the pitch. Goal.

One of his teammates came over and clapped him on the back. "That was awesome."

He smiled. "Thanks."

Then he turned around and saw Cole was standing behind him, glaring. He certainly wasn't smiling any more.

Chapter Eight

I woke up feeling exhausted. I'd slept badly again.
Yet another broken night. My eyes flickered open as
pieces of my dreams came to me. Mum of course.
It was always about Mum. Instinctively I reached
out for the glass of water that I usually kept on my
bedside table, but instead I just touched thin air.

"You knocked it over last night."

The voice made me jump. Dad? What the hell
was he doing here?

I opened my eyes. That took effort. A dull pain
was pressing behind them. I often woke up with
headaches like this when I hadn't slept well. I really
wanted to roll over and pull the duvet back over my
head.

Dad didn't look happy. "What were you doing last night?"

"Urgh?" My tongue felt fat and dry. I needed water.

"*What were you doing last night*?" He said the words slower this time, leaning in towards me. He had a hard look on his face. He was obviously really stressed out.

"I was out with a friend."

"Until ten o'clock. And then you came in without a word."

"I was just out – that's all."

I remembered nicking the chocolate and my stomach began to roll inside me. God, what if Dad found out about that? He really would kill me.

"So now you're lying." His eyes were blazing as if he really could read my mind.

"I'm not lying," I muttered, hating myself.

"It's not good enough, Alfie. You can't come back late like that, not even tell me where you were. I was worried."

"So why didn't you say anything when I came in?"

Why, instead, did you grunt at me when I walked through the door and then stomp into your own room like you hated me. What was that all about?

84

"I was angry, Alfie. I didn't want to say the wrong thing," he said coolly.

I sat up straight to face him. "Dad, it was one night. One night where I was late back and forgot to call you first. When do I ever do anything wrong? I'll still go to school. I'll still do what I'm meant to do. Why get so stressed over it?"

He sighed. I could see I'd got him there. After all, he was always saying that I didn't go out enough, that I'd shut myself away. He couldn't really complain now.

"OK," he said softly. "Have a shower. Get dressed. I'll run you to school. That way you won't be late."

"You don't have to take me," I said.

"Oh, yes. Yes I do," he replied stiffly.

And that was his way of telling me that he felt he had to.

It was clear that he still didn't trust me.

We didn't talk much in the car. Dad flicked on Radio 2, as usual, and I sat back, holding in a groan as the presenter filled the tight space of the car with his endless drone. Then a song came on, something old and guitar-based, and Dad started hitting the steering wheel in time with the beat.

"You used to like this one," he said.

"No, I didn't," I muttered back. But the song *did* start to sound familiar, once it kicked in. A warm memory trickled through me, of Dad playing the song when I was younger, of both of us jumping around the room like weirdos and mum being there, laughing. Calling us idiots. Telling us to put something decent on.

I closed my eyes.

"You did. Oasis. You used to sing along."

I could feel the words nudging at my brain now, tiny fragments like splinters embedded there.

"I don't remember it," I said eventually, and I heard him sigh.

His hands stopped hitting the wheel.

The song seemed too loud all of a sudden, seemed to go on too long. I fidgeted in my seat, still struggling with the headache that burned behind my eyes.

"You'll be OK today?" he asked as we pulled up outside the school.

I undid my belt. Opened my door. "I'll be fine."

"And you'll come straight home? I won't be late tonight."

I looked across at him and bit back the sarcastic *makes a change* comment that was desperate to fly out of my mouth. He looked different today, like he wanted to say more. He seemed smaller somehow, which seemed a crazy thought to have about Dad – he's such a big guy. Normally.

"I won't be late," I said finally.

"Good." His hand moved across the wheel. "We need to get back on track, don't we?"

Back on track? I carried on staring at him. He smiled weakly then spoke again.

"Alfie, I was thinking. When you get home later, maybe we could spend some time together. We could watch the match on TV?"

I froze. This wasn't like him. Why did he suddenly want to spend time with me? What was this? Sudden guilt?

This was too alien. Too unfamiliar. Something tugged inside of me. Was I even ready for this?

After all, he still wouldn't talk to me. He'd still act like everything was OK. What was the point of pretending all the time? I couldn't carry on doing that. I just couldn't.

"I don't know, Dad. I might be busy," I said, ducking out of the door.

I wanted you before – remember? Where were you then, eh?

Where were you then?

"Alfie – I just think—

"No. I'm fine. Honestly. Leave it."

I quickly slammed the door shut before he could say anything else.

It was much too late now.

I walked up the path and waited until the car pulled away before I made my way back to the main gates. I was looking for Alice. For some reason, I really wanted to see her.

I leant up against the gatepost. The tiny piece of toast that Dad had made me eat was not sitting well in my stomach. I watched as crowds of students pushed past, barely noticing me. My eyes scanned through them, hoping to see her. This was probably the gate she would come through, but what if she came through the back instead? Or what if she didn't come to school? My mind started to wander. What if her Mum had found out what we had done? She could be on the phone now, complaining about some year eight boy who had led her girl astray. I rubbed my head, as if that could clear all the thoughts away. Nobody would believe that it was her idea in the first place.

Why hadn't I talked her out of it? Why had I been so stupid?

"You look as bad as I feel."

I turned around. She was standing right behind me, still wearing that thin denim jacket, and her dark hair looking wilder than before, if that was even possible. I fleetingly wondered if she ever brushed it.

"Are you all right?" I asked. "I felt bad yesterday, leaving you to walk home. But I had to get back. I was so late already."

"I was fine. How was your dad in the end?"

I groaned. "Just annoying – like usual."

Her eyes glinted. "So, what do you fancy doing today?"

I shifted on the spot, not sure what she meant. "Well, there's school and then I have to be home straight away because my dad is on my case."

"Are you OK though?" she asked. "I mean you look pretty rough."

I shrugged. "I didn't sleep well, that's all. I woke up with a bad headache."

Her grin widened. "Then maybe you shouldn't be in school? You do look really ill. Maybe you need some fresh air? Be somewhere different?"

I hesitated. "I don't think—"

"Can you really face school today?"

"No . . . but—"

She grabbed my hand. "So . . . come on."

I pulled back a little, still not sure. There was no one around the gate now; everyone was filing into school. It was time to go in. I always went in.

"Come *on*," she said again, and I found myself following her out of the gate and away from everyone else. A prickle of excitement lit up inside of me.

"Where are we going?" I asked.

She smiled back at me. "On an adventure."

He didn't like today. Everyone was uneasy. Dad was worried. He kept asking Mum questions, checking that she was sure.

"It's only two degrees out there, Julia. Is this a good idea?"

Each time, she told him he was being silly.

"I'm fine. You have to believe it. You can't keep treating me like a fragile doll."

She did look better, that was true. It had been months since her last treatment in hospital. The colour was returning to her cheeks and she was putting on weight again. She wasn't too frail to hug. She no longer spent days hidden away in her room.

He was scared too, of course. This was a big match — the cup final. And of course he wanted his mum there. But he didn't want her to get ill again either.

Nothing would stop her, though.

"I've missed enough of your games, Alfie, and I plan to be at every one now," she said. "Besides, I'm hoping you might even score for me today."

In the car, Dad cranked up the radio and Mum sang along to the rubbish song that was playing. Usually this would make him cringe, but today it was making him smile. This was all good.

He was nervous as they got to the grounds. This was a big deal. They were going to play the biggest team in the county, unbeaten in twelve games. He glanced back at his smiling parents, at his mum looking so strong and healthy. Taking a deep breath, he ran across the field to his team.

It was a tough game. Within minutes they were a goal down. Rushfield's heads were starting to drop, they were losing pace and Cole was getting angry up front. But then Alfie picked up the ball on the wing. He had loads of space. He ran, whipping the ball across the face of the goal where it met Cole's boot perfectly. He squared it into the back of the net.

One-all.

"Nice one, mate," said Cole, punching him on the arm.

The game got tighter, with both teams making attempts to score. It looked as though it might be a draw, but with minutes to go, he picked up the ball just past the halfway line. Looking up, he spotted the goalie off his line. Could he do it? Was it too risky?

Without any more thinking, he chipped the ball and watched as it curved perfectly over the keeper's head.

The small crowd roared. Cole and the others ambushed him in amazement.

"Mate, that was awesome!"

"What a goal!"

But all he could hear, above the cheers and the shouts, was his mum's voice screaming his name.

She was there.

She had seen.

Because suddenly that was all that mattered.

Chapter Nine

Alice was walking so fast that I could barely keep up. She kept looking behind her shoulder, as if she was paranoid that we were about to get caught, but I felt strangely calm about the whole thing. There was no way I felt up to being in school, so anything was better than sitting in a stuffy classroom. What did one day matter anyway? Was I allowed to break the rules for once?

"So, where are we going?" I asked again, pretty sure that Alice didn't actually have a clue. We were walking along the back streets, away from the school and towards our own houses.

"Anywhere away from that place!" she said. "Honestly, I don't know how you put up with it. It's so grim."

"Aren't all schools? What was your last one like?"

Alice huffed. "I wasn't there for long, but yeah, it was pretty much the same. Teachers having a go all the time, other kids thinking they can push you around…"

"How many schools have you been to?"

"Dunno. Four, maybe? We move around a lot."

"Why?" I couldn't help asking. There was so much I didn't know about her.

Alice shook her head, avoiding my gaze. "We just do. It's how we are. Mum's not very good at settling." She stopped walking and looked up. "This is my road. Where we live for now."

"Oh yeah, your posh house!"

I looked up the road. It really was nice up here. All tall, detached Victorian houses with sweeping drives and long, neat front gardens.

Alice went quiet.

"It's really not posh," she said quietly.

"Which one is yours?"

She shuffled a bit on the spot. "Can you see the one on the right, about seven houses down as the road bends? The one with the red door."

I craned my head forward. The house was just as grand as the others. Tall and imposing with huge old-fashioned windows and a paved front garden. "It looks nice," I said.

"Does it?" Alice said. "Look a bit closer. Maybe it was nice, once. It's not *all* ours, Alfie. We're stuffed at the top in one lousy, draughty room, sharing a bathroom with a really loud family that never seem to sleep."

I looked her blankly. "What is it – some kind of guest house?"

She snorted. "It's like a B & B, or some place they shove you in when you're homeless and have nowhere else to go. It's full of families that they don't know what else to do with. It's like some kind of rubbish bin."

I looked again at the house, seeing it a bit differently now. "That sounds awful," I said finally.

"It is." She turned, facing me, her eyes gleaming. "But I don't want to talk about that. Today is about having an adventure – so let's go have one."

Between us we only had a fiver – not really enough to pay for anything exciting – but Alice didn't care.

"C'mon," she said, grabbing my hand.

We jumped the ticket barriers at the train station and leapt on to the first train that rolled into the station. It was heading towards the countryside.

"Where exactly are we going?" I asked. "When are we getting off?"

"I don't really know," Alice said. "Tell you what, we'll get off at the first stop that we fancy."

I shrugged. OK.

It was hard not to get caught up in Alice's energy. We sat ourselves at the back of the train, which was pretty quiet. There was an older lady sat on the other side reading a book and a woman with a young baby sitting across from us.

"What if a ticket inspector comes?" I whispered.

I hated sounding lame, but at the same time I didn't fancy getting thrown off the train or being landed with some huge fine that I'd have to explain away to Dad – especially when I should have been at school. That was hassle I really didn't need.

Alice shrugged. "They won't. This isn't a busy line."

"You sound like you've done this sort of thing before."

"So what if I have?"

Alice was staring out the window now, her face almost totally pressed up against the glass. I slumped back on the hard, ripped-up seat. It was strange the way Alice did this – one minute she was all happy and keen to do stuff, the next she was snappy and acting like I was annoying her.

I sighed loudly and pulled out my phone, but there wasn't much there to look at. Everyone was at school, like normal people. Right now I should be in maths with Cole kicking the back of my chair and driving me mad.

What am I even doing here? Were we seriously going to have some exciting day out in the middle of nowhere? It's freezing. We have no cash and I barely know this girl.

Who even is she?

"What's the deal with you, Alice?" I said finally.

She turned to face me, looking totally confused.

"I mean, you turned up out of nowhere, and we've been hanging out but never at school. I . . . I don't really know you. So what's going on with you? Who are you really?"

She looked back outside again. "I *told* you. We move around a lot. And I'm not *into* school."

"*No one* is into school. Show me someone who loves it."

"Yeah, well. My mum—"

She stopped suddenly and looked back over at me. I swear her eyes were filling up. She quickly rubbed them with her sleeve, like she couldn't bear for me to see, and then returned her gaze to the window.

"What about your mum?" I asked, pressing her.

"It's complicated. You wouldn't understand."

"Why wouldn't I?"

She tipped up her chin and sniffed hard. "How *could* you? Look at you – you're just like the rest of them. You pretend you have it hard, but you know nothing about what that really means. You sulk around, acting like everything is so tough. . ."

I sucked in a breath, not sure what to say.

She shook her head. "I'm sorry. I didn't mean that."

But she'd said it now, the words were out there. "Why do you think I've got it so easy?" I asked.

"Because people like you always have. I've seen it all before. I've hung around with others who moan about their lives. *My mum is sooo mean, my dad won't buy me the new iPhone. Like – poor, poor me.*" She snorted. "It's pathetic."

I whistled low. "*Wow.* Nice that you shove everyone into the same box."

Her cheeks were going red. "It's just what I've seen. That's all."

"So why did you want to hang around with me then? If I'm just another loser?"

She shrugged. "It's something to do."

I shook my head. I couldn't believe she'd made these assumptions about me; she was seriously out of order. What gave her the right to think like that?

"The thing is," I said, "you don't know anything about my life. Not one thing."

Her eyes drifted up towards mine, looking softer now.

"I'm sorry, Alfie," she said, finally. "I just assume that everyone is the same."

"Well, they're not."

I felt so heavy, so tired. The headache behind my eyes was getting worse; it felt like it was beginning to grind into the back of my skull. I rubbed at my forehead, wishing that I could force it away.

"I'm sorry," she said again.

"But what's going on with you that you judge everyone else so badly?" I said finally. "Is it really that awful for you?"

"Yes," she said softly. "But I don't want to talk about it. I want to have fun and not think about it for a bit."

I shook my head again. This was all so crazy.

Alice suddenly gripped my hand and squeezed it really tight.

"I *will* tell you, Alfie. One day, I'll explain

everything. Just not today. Is that OK?"

Her eyes fixed on mine. Wide and clear, they looked – well, they looked almost scared. I'd not seen her like this before.

"All right. . ." I sighed. "But no more acting like you know all about me. Because you don't."

She nodded. "Fair enough."

We felt the train starting to slow down. Above us the announcement system announced that we were coming into Hornsgreen.

"You ever been to Hornsgreen?" Alice asked.

"Never."

"Well, you are today," she grinned.

I forced myself to smile back, trying to ignore the uneasy feelings swimming inside of me.

What really was going on with Alice?

The sunflower had already started to grow.

He knelt on the ground to inspect it. Eight months and he could already see the stalk shooting up from the dark, compacted earth. Gently he touched the delicate stem.

"You'll grow so tall," he whispered. "You have to. Taller than me."

It was peaceful today. Even outside in the garden the birds seemed quieter than usual. It was weird, and slightly unnerving. Like the world was on edge, just waiting.

Slowly he picked himself up from the ground and dusted off the loose bits of mud and grit. Mum didn't like him being dirty. She didn't like it being brought into the house. And today everything had to be perfect.

Inside, Granddad was waiting, sitting in front of the

TV, although it was pretty obvious that he wasn't actually watching it. His hands were tapping on his legs. It was a thing he did when he was nervous.

"All right, son?"

His voice was bright, but there was a wobble there. Alfie nodded back. He didn't want to talk. He had so many questions but he was too scared to ask them. He was scared of what he might be told.

"They shouldn't be too long now. . ."

Alfie's eyes darted towards the clock. Was Granddad right? Would they be home soon? It had been hours. He wasn't supposed to know that this was an important visit, but he'd overheard Mum and Dad talking last night. He knew today was the day that they found out whether Mum was going to get better or not.

He sunk down on the floor next to Granddad. He wasn't sure how long he was there for, but it was comforting having his hair gently stroked.

Please let it be OK.

Please let it be OK.

Please. . .

When the front door finally creaked open, he found he couldn't move. His legs were heavy with cramp and his stomach was twisted in the tightest of knots. So he kept still. Waiting. Feeling Granddad lift himself out of the *chair behind him, seeing him walk into the hall. Listening to the hushed voices beyond the door.*

He squeezed his eyes shut.

Please let it be OK.

Please let it be OK.

She crept into the room and crouched down beside him. He felt her head nestle in beside his own. Her breath was soft against his cheek.

"Alfie. . ."

He couldn't open his eyes, so he shook his head instead, and kept shaking it. He was so hopelessly scared, and he knew if he looked at her — if he saw her face — he would know the truth. And he wasn't sure if he was ready for that.

"Alfie." She tugged his shoulder a little. "Alfie, look at me."

He finally lifted his head. It was like a lead ball. His eyes fluttered open and looked into hers. They were glistening with tears, just like his.

"Alfie. It's OK. I'm beating it. The cancer hasn't spread. I'm going to be OK."

He could barely speak. "You're going to be OK?"

"Yes. Yes, I promise."

She pulled him into a hug and held him so tight that he could barely breathe, but he didn't care. She was going to be fine. She had promised now.

The nightmare was over.

Chapter Ten

It was pretty clear as soon as we stepped outside of the station that Hornsgreen was in the middle of nowhere. The station itself was two platforms with a small ticket booth and an ancient-looking vending machine. There was no one around at all; the place looked completely deserted.

"The exit is that way," Alice said, dragging me towards the bridge.

"This place is *dead*," I said, checking behind me. I half expected some guy to jump out of the ticket booth and shout at us, but there was no movement inside. "We could just wait here for another train. Go back again?"

Her eyes shone. "What would be the point of that?"

"I dunno. This place seems dull."

"So what? No one knows us here. That's all that counts," she replied.

I wasn't so sure. Was this really better than school? I mean, don't get me wrong, I hate the place. But at least it keeps me busy. And to be fair, it's where I was meant to be.

This felt all wrong.

Alice started to walk towards the bridge, her huge bag slung over her shoulder. "C'mon!" she yelled.

I followed like her little lapdog over the old iron structure that was turning to rust. As we crossed over the top, I cast my eyes over the view. I guess it was quite pretty. On one side there were rolling fields and trees, on the other there was a windy road and a cluster of buildings, which I assumed was the village itself.

We went through a tiny gate that led down a thin side street and came out on to the windy road I'd seen up above. We both looked around. This place was really tidy. Every house was neatly tucked away from the road, with a front garden overloaded with colourful plants. There was no litter. No graffiti. Hardly any noise at all.

"This is dead posh," said Alice.

I nodded. "It's really nice." I was still looking around me, taking it all in. Each house looked individual, and well looked after. The gardens were just awesome.

"My mum would've liked it here," I said without thinking.

Alice's ears were sharp. "Would've? What, she wouldn't like it now then?"

I sighed. There was no way round this. I obviously couldn't keep avoiding the subject.

"No. She's dead."

"Oh." Alice's expression changed, but only a little. It was almost as if she was mindful not to make a big deal about it. She flapped her hand loosely instead. "I shouldn't have asked, sorry."

"It's all right."

It wasn't though. Just being here, in this peaceful pretty village, was making me feel so sad. I should be here with my mum.

I shouldn't be here with someone like Alice.

But what else was I going to do? I was here now. I had to make the best of it.

Like I always did.

*

We had eaten two mars bars, some cheap cola and a jumbo bag of onion fries between us. This wasn't exactly what I had in mind, but I didn't care any more. I was cold and tired, and I wanted to go home, but I couldn't tell Alice that. I didn't want her thinking that I was boring or pathetic.

We were sitting in a small green area by a lake, fairly hidden by the trees and largely ignored by the few people that walked past us. I casually flicked through my phone. There still wasn't much going, but I saw a message from Ben. I opened it up, feeling a bit uneasy.

Hey. Where are you? Need to catch up soon, dude.

I felt a bit sad reading. It had been quite cool spending time with Ben, getting to know him again, and now I was slacking off school to be with this strange new girl. I wasn't even sure I liked her much.

I took a gulp of cola and felt the fizz burn at the back of my throat. This was all just an excuse. I was only with Alice because it was easier than being with people I knew. People who *knew me*.

I shoved my phone back into my pocket. I'd deal with Ben later. I wasn't sure I was ready to hear about his ongoing love obsession anyway. Alice had her head tipped back towards the sky. She looked like she was lost in her thoughts. She looked almost peaceful.

"Look up at the clouds, Alfie," she said, pointing.

I looked up. The sky was a deep blue and there were some large white clouds drifting above us. Nothing special, though.

"What about them?"

"Look at the *shapes*," she said. "Really *look*. They're like faces."

I squinted my eyes. "Nah. I can't see it."

"They do!" she practically shouted. "Look at that one! Just above us. It has a bit sticking out, like a long nose. It looks like Miss Yeats."

I snorted. Good job Ben wasn't with us. She's his favourite teacher.

"And that one." She pointed over to the left. "It has huge ears, like Dumbo."

I shook my head a little. "I guess..." I couldn't really see what she was seeing. They looked like white cotton-wool balls to me.

"You have no imagination," she muttered.

"Obviously!"

"Look again!"

So I did. I squinted my eyes and tried to see what she could. The white swirls moved above me, almost making me feel dizzy. But there was one shape. A small tangle of white that was drifting to the right. It had a face-like look. I nudged Alice.

"There, that one. I can see a weird-looking face over there."

She smiled. "Yes! See!"

"In fact, it looks a bit like you."

She snorted and nudged me hard in the ribs. "My head is not that shape."

I hadn't been aware of someone standing there but when I tipped my head forward, there he was – a guy standing right in front of us. He was pretty old, with a hard look held on his wide, pudgy face. He had a small black dog on a lead that looked similar to the clouds, actually – just a mass of fluff. The dog sniffed my feet and then lifted his head and looked at me accusingly.

"Can I help you?" I asked, because I didn't know what else to say. Why was this bloke so close to us? And why was he letting his dog sniff us like that?

"Shouldn't you both be in school?" the man replied, and his voice was polite but firm.

Alice's attention was immediately drawn away from the sky. She turned to the man. I didn't like the look on her face. She had a nasty snarl and her eyes were gleaming.

"What's it to you?" she spat.

"It's everything to do with me if I believe you are truanting," the man replied. He was still very calm.

"We have an INSET Day," I shot back.

The man scanned us, and I was suddenly aware that he could see my uniform sticking out from under my coat. I tried to pull it tighter to me.

"What school do you go to?"

"St Nicholas," I replied. There was no point in lying. Besides, we were in another town. This guy wouldn't have a clue if I was right or not.

The man nodded. "Interesting, because I'm sure St Nicholas doesn't have an INSET today."

Alice shifted on the bench. I could almost feel her rage. "And what the hell would *you* know?"

The man stepped back a little. "It's a confident guess."

That made Alice even more annoyed. She jumped out of her seat.

"You're bang out of order! Coming over here and having a go. We're not bothering you. Just go away and leave us alone."

"I think the school would be very interested to know what you are up to."

"It's none of your business!" Alice was almost shouting now. I turned my head away; my cheeks were burning. This was really embarrassing.

The man shook his head sadly at both of us. I swear he was staring more at me. Like he was really disappointed in me.

"Just go! And take your smelly, ugly-faced dog with you," she shouted after him.

The man's face turned bright red. "You are an extremely rude girl!" he snapped.

"And you are a fat, nosy old man!"

There was a brief silence before Alice sat herself back down on the bench. Her eyes were still blazing. I wanted to say something but didn't in case I wound her up again. But I knew that *she* was the one who'd been bang out of order. He was just an old bloke. You didn't speak to people like that. It wasn't right.

"I hope you'll think about your actions today," the man said, turning to walk away. His voice was softer now, and a bit shaky.

"I will," I mumbled.

I couldn't bring myself to look at Alice, but I could hear her muttering under her breath.

The warm feeling inside me had definitely gone.

It was amazing how quickly time passed, how everything seemed to grow in a blink of an eye.

Before long he was as tall as his mum, and the sunflower in the garden was taller than him. Mum would stand outside and stare up at it with pure pleasure on her face.

"I never thought it would take," she said. "But it did. Everything just worked out."

Routines slotted back into place. Dad was back at work again, so it was mainly just him and her. He liked that though. He liked that she was busy again, out in the garden or painting the house.

It wasn't just the sunflower growing; she was too. But in a different way.

"It changes you," she told him. "Cancer makes you look at everything differently. You appreciate what you have far, far more. And we have so much."

Today she was gardening again. It was her favourite thing to do. She said she found it soothing, and sometimes he did too.

"You have so much to look forward to," she said. "Look at you – you'll be at secondary school next year and you have trials lined up." She smiled. "You're going to be a superstar."

He shifted uneasily. This was the one thing that weighed heavily on him. He knew how proud they were of his football. It made them both so happy. But it also scared him.

"What if I mess it up, Mum?"

She shook her head. Her curls had grown back now and they bounced gently against her face.

"You won't mess up."

"I might."

Only last weekend he'd missed a clear chance at a goal and then had trouble taking the ball from other players. He'd been slow and clumsy. The team had had a right go at him. Especially Cole. Afterwards he wondered if everyone was wrong about him – if they were kidding themselves that he was some great player when actually he was nothing special.

"You won't mess up," she said again, and her voice was firmer now. "Alfie, as long as you give everything your *best shot, you won't mess up. It doesn't matter if you make the trials or not. We just want you to be happy, to be proud of yourself."*

He felt his head dip. "I only want to make you happy."

"Well, then you are messing up," she said softly. "This is your life. Your shot at it. Don't worry about me."

She pulled him tight into a hug. "I'll always be proud of you, Alfie. And whatever you end up doing, I'll be there supporting you."

He believed her.

Chapter Eleven

We barely spoke on the way back. Alice kept moaning about the day being ruined. I was more concerned about the man she'd upset. What if he reported us? He knew what school we went to.

"You worry too much," she teased.

And, yeah, maybe I did. But I seriously didn't want a load of hassle about why I missed school and why I was hanging around in a park out of town. I knew the school would be worried and I didn't want them to be. If they worried then they would start to question me again. If they questioned me again they might ask to me to consider counselling again.

And there was no way. No way I was going back down that route.

I was fine. This was just a stupid mistake.

We had to hang around the station for ages waiting for a train. I kept checking my watch nervously. I needed to get home before Dad. Questions from school would be bad, but questions from him would be far worse.

"Why are you so moody?" she asked finally, coming up close to me. Too close.

I glared at her. "Are you for real? This was such a rubbish idea. We've wasted an entire day hanging around in some dead-end village and the grand finale was you screaming in the face of some old geezer."

Alice sucked her teeth. "Exaggeration! I just shouted a bit, that's all. I hardly screamed in his face."

"It was full on. You were really loud," I said.

A small, nasty grin crept across her face. "Seriously? Listen to you. And here's me thinking you might be different."

I turned towards her. "Different? In what way?"

"I don't know, a bit more carefree. Someone who's happy to have a little fun and not stick to the rules for once."

I wasn't even sure how to answer that. I just carried on glaring at her. "You don't even know me."

"No, clearly not," she sniffed. "You're obviously

just some loser who's angry at life because his mum's dead."

I froze, my eyes locked on hers. She still had a tight smile on her face. She was testing me. I knew it. She wanted me to lose my temper, to totally lose control.

I am sad, yes. And I am a loser too.

I've lost everything.

But I'm not admitting that to you. I'm not admitting that to anyone.

I'm not making it any more real.

"Go on, Alfie. Tell me! Tell me how bad it is for you. Stop looking at me with those sad eyes." She shook her head. "Get angry. Shout at me. Tell me what you're thinking!"

No. No. I'm not doing that.

The feelings raged and bubbled inside of me.

I had to push it away before it choked me. Before it exploded.

"And you'd know, wouldn't you?" I hissed. "You'd know about angry feelings."

Her eyes sparkled. "What do you mean?"

"Well, look at you – homeless, right? Living in one room because you're too poor to get a place of your own. Sounds like you must be feeling pretty angry too. I know I would be if I had nothing like you."

She was still staring back at me. Her eyes locked on mine. I saw something flicker there – what was it? Hurt? Confusion? Very slowly she shook her head.

You went too far, Alfie.

I swallowed, regret swamping me. "Alice. I shouldn't have—"

But her eyes were cold.

"Stay away from me," she hissed.

Then she turned on her heels and walked away, leaving me alone on the platform.

The house was dark as he walked towards it. I was pleased. My mouth tasted of stale cola and cheap onion fries. My stomach and head were aching. Above all, I just wanted to lay on my bed and sleep. It was still early, around six p.m., but I seriously felt like I could go to bed and sleep right through the night.

I kept thinking about Alice. I felt conflicted. Part of me was still fed up with her. She was like some kind of overgrown kid with a big gob. But another part of me felt guilty. I'd left her by herself in some deserted station. OK, it wasn't dark and it was her that decided to storm off, but, even so, that wasn't a cool thing to do. And, stupidly, I didn't even have her number, so I couldn't text her to check that she was all right.

What was wrong with me? Why was I acting like such an idiot all the time?

I shoved the key in the lock and walked inside. It all seemed quiet. Throwing my bag in the hall, I went to go in the kitchen. I decided that eating something – even if it was just a slice of toast – might actually help with my stomach ache. But only sleep would help with my head and I needed that more and more.

Suddenly I noticed Dad emerging slowly out of the living room. Weirdly, he looked bigger than ever. His huge, meaty arms were crossed in front of him and his face was expressionless. Even so, I knew he was angry. I knew I was in trouble. I could feel a heap of excuses tumble into my brain but none of them sounded good enough. What was the point, anyway? He was going to have a go no matter what I said.

I stepped back and stared up at his face. Tried to make myself feel as big as him. He wasn't going to intimidate me.

"Why didn't you go to school?"

I kept my cool. "How do you know?"

"They text me, don't they?" he snorted. "Did you seriously think you'd get away with it? That school is hot on attendance, Alfie. They want me to call them and tell them where you were."

I frowned back at him. He could do what he wanted for all I cared.

"Maybe I shouldn't bother. Maybe I should let them ask you."

"If you want."

He banged a fist against his leg. "Stop being lippy. Just tell me what's going on. Where *were* you?"

"What's it to you?"

As soon as I said it, I knew that I sounded like her – like Alice. But there was something powerful in challenging him. After all, why *should* he care? Why *now*? Dad drew a deep breath. I knew he was composing himself, trying not to let his anger out. He wasn't very good at hiding it.

"Don't speak to me like that," he said, struggling to keep his voice level. "I asked you a question. Now answer me. Why weren't you at school?"

I shrugged. "I just didn't fancy it."

"You *just didn't fancy it*?" he mimicked.

"Yeah? And?" I was getting stressed now. I didn't like him taking the mickey out of me.

"So you decided you'd take the day off and hang around like some layabout?"

"I'm *not* a layabout."

"You'll end up like one if you carry on like this." He was shaking his head, his cheeks turning redder and redder by the second.

I scowled at him. "Seriously. I don't know what your problem is. It was one day. ONE. DAY—"

"Don't you DARE shout at me!"

His hand flew up. It was inches away – just inches away from my face. I could see it shaking in mid-air. Then he brought it back down again, and he was still for a second, like he couldn't quite believe what he'd done.

I wasn't sure what to do at first. He'd never gone that far before. He'd shouted. He'd thrown angry words my way. But he'd never gone to hit me.

And I don't know why, but I laughed. It just slipped out. It was so weird seeing him there, this big man who was trying to act all tough with me. But he couldn't do it. He couldn't bring himself to actually hurt me. All he could do was chuck words at my face and try to scare me with useless threats. That was typical of him. Leaving things unfinished.

He looked at me, like he could quite believe my reaction, and he shook his head.

"I don't understand you any more," he said. "If

your mum was here—"

"If Mum was here *what*?" I asked him.

But he said nothing. He just shook his head again and walked away. "We'll talk later. I'm done."

"No!" I yelled at his back. "If my mum was here, then *what*? What would be different?"

He slammed the door.

"Would we be happy?" I yelled through the wood. "Would we be a *normal family*?"

His music went on. Loud.

"If Mum was here, would she *listen to me*?" I screamed. "Would she actually *notice I was here*?"

I pressed my nose up against the door. My head was killing now and I was feeling really sick.

"Why didn't you talk, Dad?" I whispered. "Why didn't you talk to me after it happened?"

But the music thumped on. Yet again he'd shut me out. The door stood between us. There was no getting through to him. He probably wouldn't speak to me now for the rest of the week.

I didn't cry for as long this time. Ten minutes, maybe a bit longer. But it still left me exhausted and drained. I buried my head deep in the pillow, breathing in the salty, cotton scent.

Downstairs I could hear the continual thump of Dad's music. I wondered what else he was doing down there. Cooking? Watching football? Reading the news? Whatever it was, *he* wouldn't be crying. Dad wouldn't be seen dead doing something as shameful as that.

I thought back to Mum's funeral. One of the darkest, longest days of my life. Even now, thinking about it made my entire stomach twist.

I had been broken. I could barely stand. I had to be held up my granddad. I remember how every movement – every word almost – made me feel like I was falling apart. I was like one of those dandelions in the breeze, clinging on the ground whilst my seeds were being pulled from my stem. Soon there'd be nothing left. I'd be bare and exposed. I had never felt so vulnerable. All I could do was stay as silent and still as I could. That seemed to control the trembling. But nothing could stop the tears that were forcing their way out of me in loud, clumsy bursts.

Dad had been so different. He'd been calm and in control. Everyone had remarked on how *brave* and *strong* he was. He stood tall, his face unreadable, his voice level.

But when he saw me sniffing in church, his hand

had swept over my lap. His face turned dark and cold.

"Don't cry. Don't make it worse."

I had to turn away from him, dip my head out of his view. Force it back. I did everything I could to keep those tears inside and I never allowed him to see me like that again.

Because Dad couldn't stand to see me weak.

And after that day I could barely stand to see him at all.

She understood. She always did. All she had to do was sit next to him and gently take his hand, and he knew she was listening.

"He winds me up," he muttered. "He always has a go. Nothing I do is good enough."

"That's not true. He's so proud of you. He just doesn't know how to show it, that's all."

He turned to face her, his eyes blazing. "If that's the case, why does he always pick holes in everything? He had a go about my school report because it wasn't one-hundred per cent excellent. Last night at training, he shouted because I wasn't fast enough..."

She squeezed his hand gently. "I think he's under a lot of stress at the moment. He just wants you to do well."

"I wish he was more like you."

She giggled, her face lighting up. "I'll tell him that!"

Her fingers stretched over his hand, gently stroking the skin. "We are completely different people, but that's why it works so well. I'm the dreamer, the optimist, and your dad—"

"Is miserable?"

"No!" She sat up. Released his hand. "No. I don't want you to say things like that. Your dad is the strong one, the realist, the fighter. Without him. . ."

Her words broke away.

He felt bad. He could see he'd upset her. He shifted on the seat uncomfortably, not really sure what he could say to make it better.

"You both mean everything to me," she whispered.

He nodded. He knew that.

"When I was sick before, I really struggled. Usually I'm so positive and upbeat. But I couldn't be then. I felt like my world had been torn apart. But it was your dad who made me see that I wasn't fighting anything alone. He made me feel strong again."

He could feel tears biting at his eyes. "Dad hated you being ill."

"I know. It was hard on all of us. But do you know what he said that made me feel so much better?"

He shook his head. He didn't.

"He said, 'Every day we have is a blessing, because we

are blessed to have so much love.'" She blinked hard, her bottom lip wobbling. "Do you see, Alfie? He feels blessed. We are so lucky to have each other."

"But what if he doesn't feel like that about me?"

"Alfie, he loves you too much. One day, you'll understand that."

Chapter Twelve

I'd been worrying about Alice all night, and after slamming out of the empty house that morning, I wondered whether I should walk past her street to see if she was there. I decided not to, worried that I might look like some obsessive stalker. Also, would Alice even want to see me? Did I want to see her? Our last conversation hadn't exactly ended well. I told myself that Alice was a million times more streetwise than me and would have got herself home fine. She would probably be quite amused to see how worried I was. She didn't strike me as the type who stressed about stuff like that. But what type *was* she? Someone who missed school to hang out in a park. I guess that was a laugh for some people once or twice, but

Alice seemed like she might be the type to do it more often.

These thoughts pricked at me as I made my way to school, and I decided to knock for Ben. I'd hardly seen him recently and I suddenly realized how much I missed being around him. But when I got to his house, his mum was already on her way to work.

"You missed him," she called out. "He left early. He's doing a project or something?"

I thanked her and carried on walking, trying not to smile. So Ben was still going in early to impress Becky. He was *seriously* deluded. I walked to school really slowly, my legs protesting the whole way. I had zero energy. Once again, my sleep had been restless and broken and I'd found myself wide-awake at five a.m., listening to Dad getting ready for work. A small part of me had wondered if I should get up and talk to him. Try to sort out our issues. But when I heard him crashing about in the bathroom and humming under his breath like he didn't have a care in the world, something in me just hardened.

Why should *I* be the one to sort it out?

*

In school, I tried to be invisible, but of course that was never going to happen. My tutor, Mr Rogers, called me over after the bell went.

"So where were you yesterday? No one phoned in for you." His tone was light, but I could tell he was digging for information – he had that intense look on his face. The same one he pasted on whenever he asked if I was *OK* or *coping*. He seemed to be able to turn his concerned look on and off like a switch. It was quite a skill.

I shrugged. "My dad forgot. I had a stomach ache."

"Oh, right." His fingers lightly drummed the papers in front of him.

"I'll get him to write a note," I said, even though there wasn't much chance of that happening. Still, I wanted Mr Rogers off my back.

"Or you could. . ." His words hung in the air for a moment. "You could just tell us the truth?"

"The truth?" I blinked and made my eyes go all wide and innocent. "I've told you. I was sick. No big deal."

"But you weren't, were you?" Mr Rogers said softly. He looked sadder now, like he could really see what was going through my mind. Like he felt sorry for me.

In that moment I could feel a cold sweat creeping up the back of my neck.

"I don't know what you mean, sir," I muttered.

"You need to report to Mrs Dennis at the end of the day," he said finally. He shook his head, like he was defeated.

"Mrs Dennis?" The head? That was a bit much, surely?

He sighed again and ran a hand through his messy hair. "Alfie, word of advice, next time you skive off school, be careful who you abuse in the street."

My stomach dropped. The old guy.

"That wasn't even me..." I said.

"Unfortunately for you, he was in here first thing and was quite able to identify you and another student."

"But it wasn't me..."

Mr Rogers came towards me, his hands held out. "This isn't like you. You know I'm worried – I wish you'd just—"

"I'm fine. This was just a mistake, that's all."

"So it's nothing to do with how you've been feeling?"

He was really annoying me now – trying to make me talk. I almost wanted to punch him. I wanted him gone and out of my face.

"Alfie, you can't keep ignoring this. Your grades are slipping. I don't see you around your old mates. Your football—"

"Seriously, sir. I'm fine," I said, grabbing my bag.

But as I left the classroom, I couldn't help thinking that I would've been a whole lot better if I had never met Alice.

I couldn't see Ben in the canteen at first. Then I spotted him sitting with a load of people from his music group. He seemed to be in deep discussion with a guy called Jenson, who I didn't know very well, but what I did know was that he always had a moody look on his face. Like he was about to break into a fight with someone. Ben said he was just "really into his music".

I never really felt comfortable with that lot. They were always talking about music, and stuff I didn't know about. It made me feel like a bit of an idiot.

As I got closer, I realized that the only spare seat I could see was next to Cole. He was sitting with Declan and Kieron from the school football team. I hesitated for a second but strolled over. This was where I used to sit every lunchtime. A tug of familiarity pulled at me.

I used to belong here... With them.

"All right?" I said as I sat down opposite them.

Cole looked up at me, a slightly surprised expression on his face, but then he nodded and smiled. "Mate. Where were you yesterday?"

"Sick," I replied

Cole snorted. "Oh *yeah*, course you were. Gracie Russell said she saw you walk out of the gate with that new girl. The weird one in the year below."

Kieron was assessing me with a bored expression. We used to get on OK, a while back, but he seemed to be more arrogant than ever now. It probably didn't help that he had taken my place on the school team. He wasn't even as good. Most of the time he just scuffed the ball. "Which weird girl is this then?" he asked. "New girlfriend?"

I felt a prickle of anger. "She's not weird, she's just..."

But what *was* she? Angry? Individual? Annoying?

"So where *were* you yesterday?" Kieron asked, obviously intrigued.

"I just wanted a day out of school, that's all. We hung around. Chilled out."

Kieron sniggered. "Sounds like fun. Seriously though, who is this girl?"

"She's in the year below," Cole told him. "Apparently she's all hair and talk. I heard she's got into loads of grief already for gobbing back at the teachers."

"She sounds great," Kieron said dryly.

Cole shook his head. "You've always been weird with girls. Remember when Faye West had it bad for you? You just ran, man."

I glared at him. "I didn't run. It wasn't a good time."

It had actually been a few weeks after Mum died, and I obviously hadn't been in the mood for flirting. I hadn't really in the mood for anything.

"It's never a good time any more though, is it?" Cole muttered, his eyes fixed on mine.

Declan nudged him, warning him to leave me alone. I liked Declan. He wasn't so gobby and seemed more on my level.

"*What?*" Cole rounded on Declan in mock horror, his hands up in defence. "I'm not being out of order. I'm just *saying*... Alf is different now. I miss him, that's all."

I looked at my lunch tray and shoved a dry chip in my mouth, chewing it while I looked at Cole.

"Things change," I said finally.

He knew this day would be one of his favourite memories of all time. If he could bottle the feeling, he would. He'd keep it for ever.

It started with the match, which was one of the best. The winter sun was warm against his body. He felt free. He moved quickly and easily along the wing – his feet barely scuffing the ground, the ball seemed to be attached to his foot, moving effortlessly with him as he twisted and turned past defenders. He could hear the cheers as he sped past the small crowd, and his heart thumped in his chest as his foot made final contact with the ball, firing it into the top corner of the goal.

It had been so easy. So perfect.

The whistle blew and his team crowded round, hugging him, pulling him towards them. He was their star player.

Mum and Dad were both there, wrapped up warm

against the cold. He could see his mum's face, pink with cold, grinning out at him. She looked good, healthy. Alive.

It was all going to be OK. She would get better again.

They were going to be OK.

Mum told him how proud she was. Teased him for having mud on his face and caked in his hair. But she didn't really care. Even Dad seemed relaxed, rocking back on his heels and smiling down on the both of them.

"You're going to be my superstar," said his mum, and he believed her.

They took him for a meal in a local pub. He was still covered in mud and probably looked a state, but today nobody minded. They ordered three large roast dinners and sat by the open fire to eat them. The food was tasty, and he had never felt so hungry. Even Mum ate well, although a little slower than them.

"When I'm completely better, we should get a dog," she said.

Dad looked up, surprised. "Seriously?"

"Yes. Why not? A lovely girl dog. We'll name her Poppy. That's what I would have called my daughter if I'd had one."

"I'd love that, Mum," he'd said.

Dad nodded. "OK. If you want."

He smiled. This really was the best day.

Chapter Thirteen

There was a small corridor outside Mrs Dennis's office, and that was where I headed once the bell went. There was no point avoiding it, I just had to face whatever she was going to throw at me. I'd only ever been down here twice before. The first time was to pick up an attendance award and the second was after Mum died. I guess you could say I'm not the kind of kid who is normally in trouble.

As I turned the corner, I saw Alice was already sitting outside waiting. Guilt pricked at me again. I should have never have left her last night.

But she looked up at me and smiled. "All right?"

I nodded.

"They got you too, then? I was thinking I might be on my own for this."

I frowned. "Of course not. We were both as guilty." I sat on the seat next to her. "I shouldn't have left you by yourself yesterday. I'm sorry."

She shrugged. "It's OK. I can look after myself."

"Even so, it was out of order."

She grinned. "Don't beat yourself up about it. I just hung around and got the next train back. At least I didn't have to listen to you moaning."

I half nodded in acknowledgement. It was a fair point.

"So what do you think they'll do?" I asked. "Detentions?"

Alice sighed and started examining the chipped pink varnish on her nails. "I dunno. Not bothered really."

"Don't you worry about this at all? What will your mum say?"

She snorted. "She'll think the school are making a fuss about nothing. She has enough on her plate at the moment."

"Seriously?"

Alice nodded. But a tiny frown crossed her face and I wasn't so sure she meant it.

"My dad will kill me," I muttered.

"No he won't," she replied.

I inhaled. No, he probably wouldn't. But he would be disappointed in me. And somehow that was even worse.

Mrs Dennis called us both in together. She's been the head at the school for quite a while now – a short woman with spiky, dark hair and bright, piercing blue eyes that seem to see right through you. Some people say she's scary, but I always thought she was quite cool – I usually quite like her. Then again, I'm not usually in trouble.

She made us both stand in front of her, and I was suddenly really aware of my height and how gangly I was. Not being able to sit was weird and I found myself fidgeting, struggling to stay still on the spot.

"*So. . .*" she said, stretching out the word. "What exactly were you both up to yesterday? And please don't insult me by lying. I had Mr Waite in here this morning. He identified both of you."

Neither of us said anything. It was so hot in there, really stuffy, but I found myself shivering a bit.

"Do you know who Mr Waite is?" she continued.

I shook my head. I don't think Alice moved at all.

"He's one of our school governors. And he was appalled at your behaviour." Mrs Dennis's voice was wobbling now. "So can you tell me what on *earth* you were doing?"

Alice looked at the floor, not saying a thing, so that left me to speak.

"We just took a day off. It wasn't planned," I said, stammering a bit. "I couldn't face school."

Mrs Dennis raised an eyebrow, her face like ice. I'd never seen her like this before. "And whose idea was this?"

Alice was still inspecting the floor, acting all quiet and small. Not so gobby now then! I shifted on the spot; the silence was making me feel so awkward.

I sighed. "Mine, Miss. It was my idea. I persuaded Alice to go."

I don't even know why I said it. It felt right somehow. I could feel myself sag, and Alice let out a quiet breath next to me.

Mrs Dennis took a step back, crossed her arms and stared hard at me. She didn't say anything, but her expression said it all. The raised eyebrow, the curl of her lip: she didn't believe me.

"Alice, what do you have to say about this?" she said finally.

Alice's head was tipped slightly forward, so that her crazy hair fell in front of her face.

"He's right. It was Alfie's idea," she muttered.

I felt my skin glow. Even though I'd taken the blame for both of us, I was surprised how quickly Alice had gone along with it.

Mrs Dennis sighed. "I must say I'm surprised, Alice. Your mum assured me that you would start here with a clean slate. That your behaviour would be different. But this sounds like more of the same, according to the reports from your previous schools."

Alice lifted her head. Now I could see the blaze in her eyes again. "It was *his* idea," she repeated, putting emphasis was on the word *his*, like she'd had nothing at all to do with it.

Mrs Dennis turned to me, looking sad now. Disappointed, maybe.

"This doesn't sound like you, Alfie."

I shrugged. "I guess it seemed like a good idea at the time."

"Are you not happy? Is there something I can help with?" she said. Her voice was softer, probing.

Not happy? Was she kidding me? I tried to rack my brains back to when I actually *was* properly happy. Even thinking about that made my muscles tighten.

Nothing was the same any more. Why couldn't anyone understand that?

"I need to speak to you separately, tomorrow," Mrs Dennis said to Alice. "I'm worried about your attitude and your attendance is concerning. Mr Waite also identified you specifically as the one who was rude to him."

Alice was still frozen next to me. She mumbled something under her breath, but I couldn't make out what it was.

Mrs Dennis turned her attention to me.

"You've never been in trouble before," she said, "but I'll be setting up some detentions. And I will need to talk to your dad about the incident with Mr Waite. I'm worried about you, Alfie."

My dad? I shook my head automatically. "No..."

Mrs Dennis frowned. "I have to inform your dad, Alfie."

But he doesn't listen. He'll shout and ignore me, and not care about how I'm feeling. He doesn't get it. He doesn't get me.

The words blazed inside me. I could feel Alice

shifting next to me uncomfortably. I just wanted to get out of the room. Get away from all of them.

"Whatever," I said finally. "Do whatever."

I was past caring.

Outside, Alice touched my arm.

"Thank you for taking the blame," she whispered. "Really . . . thank you."

I was actually surprised she thanked me. That wasn't something I would expect from her.

"It's OK," I muttered.

"It's hard . . . with my mum," she continued, turning away from me. "I don't think she can deal with me right now."

"It's OK," I repeated, "honestly."

We started walking out of the building. I was glad to get out of there, breathe in some fresh air, shake off the stink of school.

"I guess I'm going to get into loads of trouble tomorrow," she sighed.

"I thought you said your mum wouldn't care?" I said, surprised.

Alice's head dropped a little. "Yeah, she will. . . I just kid myself that she won't. To stop feeling guilty, you know. I keeping messing stuff up and then I feel so bad after. Mum doesn't need this."

"I'm sure she'll understand."

"Nah, she will be upset. I wish I could stop letting her down," Alice said softly. She waved her hand vaguely at the school buildings. "I find this all so hard, you know . . . all this. I'm not like everyone else," she said finally. "I don't fit in. I never have."

"No," I replied. "Right now. Neither do I."

He heard them talking.

They didn't think he could, of course, but he was wide awake and he couldn't help but hear them as he crept downstairs to get some water. He'd been having trouble sleeping recently. Ever since he started secondary school. It was OK, but it was a big change. Stressful. And now football was piling on the pressure too. There was talk of an important tournament in Brighton next week, one where scouts would be watching. His dad was really excited, but he just felt anxious.

What if he messed it up? What if he let everyone down?

He stood outside the living room door, wondering if he should cough. Or just burst in. It was obvious from their hushed tones that they were discussing something serious.

But then his mum spoke, and he found that he couldn't move at all.

"Don't tell Alfie about this, not yet. I don't want to worry him."

His hand gripped into a fist. Worry? What about? Everything was meant to be OK now.

"All right," his dad replied. "He's got a lot on at the moment anyway – his football, school. . ."

"Exactly." His mum's voice sounded husky. "I don't want to affect that. I want him to have the best chance. . . I don't want to be the reason. . ."

Her voice broke, and he felt himself crumple slightly inside. She was crying.

"Oh God – what if. . .?"

Dad's voice was firm. "Don't talk that that. We don't know anything yet."

"I know." She was whispering now. "But the scan didn't look good, did it?"

There was silence. Silence. It was so thick, he could almost taste it.

"I thought I'd beaten it," she sobbed.

"Don't," his dad begged. "Just . . . don't. . ."

He stood at the closed door, staring at nothing, listening to the broken sounds of his parents crying. He didn't know how long he was there, or how he got back upstairs again. But he didn't sleep at all that night.

He knew that his mum's promise was destroyed. She would leave him.

She would leave both of them.

And then what?

Chapter Fourteen

"I don't understand it."

Dad looked beaten. I really wasn't sure what to say. I wasn't angry with him, which made a change – I just felt awkward and stupid and I really couldn't stand being next to him. Being next to him made me feel worse.

"Aren't you going to say anything? Anything at all?"

I slumped back on the sofa, my eyes glued to my phone so that I didn't have to look directly at him. "No. Not really."

"I mean – first *skipping school* and now this. Being rude to some bloody governor. Alfie... What's that all about?" He was pacing the floor in front of me.

"You *know* how important school is. You can't mess around with your life like this."

"It was a one-off. That's all. No big deal," I said.

"But was it? *Really*? I don't know how I can believe that when so much about you has changed. There's this and the moods, then there's the football. . ."

I looked up. "The football is different," I said.

"Is it, though?" His voice was softer than usual. I wasn't used to this. "Because football was *everything* to you. You loved it so much and then you just gave up on it."

"I *grew out of it*," I muttered.

"I really don't think that's true, is it, Alfie?"

Our eyes locked, and for once I felt like he was challenging me to say more. But what could I say? There was so much. So much stacked up inside me, and I didn't even know where to start. If I started, I might never stop.

Finally, he shook his head sadly and looked away.

"I get it, you know. I know why you quit. You think you're not allowed to be happy any more."

"What about you, Dad? You've been the same," I hit back. "When did you last go to a game?"

His face closed up. "This isn't about me."

"But it is, isn't it? Can't you see? It's both of us."

"Alfie – I'm not here to talk about me. I'm worried about you."

I leapt up, phone still in my hand. "You really haven't got a clue, have you?"

Dad turned to me, eyes blazing. "No, Alf! Maybe I haven't. But I'm trying here—"

"Trying? Really? Well, maybe you're not trying hard enough."

I couldn't stand to be the same room as him any longer, so I went to leave. As I did so, he called after me.

"I'm trying, Alfie. I'm trying to help you."

Help me? Seriously?

Where was he when I really needed him? When we both really needed him?

He could never help me.

He couldn't even help himself.

It took minutes for me to smash up my room. I barely knew what I was doing. I tipped the mattress, kicked over the bin. It was stupid – childish – but the rage needed to go somewhere. The trophies were next. I picked up each one and hurled them out the open window, into the back garden. Most landed in the bushes. But one – my Manager's Player of the Year –

landed right beside Mum's sunflower, which took the satisfaction away entirely.

I hated those trophies; even knowing they were still in the garden bugged me. I didn't want to see them again. They were part of the past. Part of that old me that I knew I couldn't get back. Because how could things ever go to back to the way they were?

How could I ever, ever forgive myself?

I left my room and stormed out of the house minutes later. Dad must have heard me, but he didn't call. Knowing him, he was busy locked back in his own world again. He had no time to worry about me.

I don't know what got to me more, the fact that Dad had attempted to talk to me, or the fact that he had given up halfway through again. I just wished that he would let rip and tell me what he was really thinking. Was that so hard?

Can't he see how much he's changed? I can't deal with this shell of a Dad; he's a shadow of the man I once knew. I don't know him any more; he's like a stranger.

I've lost my mum already, but sometimes it feels like I've lost my dad too.

I walked fast. Past the allotments, past the park. I knew exactly where I was heading: I was going to Alice.

The only person who seemed real at the moment. The only person who seemed as angry and as out of place as me. As I turned into her road, I looked around at the houses. This was the kind of place I'd wanted to live when I was little. The houses seemed so distinctive and homely, with proper driveways and porches. Even the street itself was nicer – the pavement was cleaner, there was no litter, and loads of trees lined the road. Alice is lucky to live here.

But as I got closer to her house, it became clear that it was set apart from the rest. I'd never really seen it this close-up before. The slabs on the driveway were broken in places, and the front garden was overgrown. Two knackered-looking bikes were leaning next to the dirty-looking front door.

I could also hear the inside noise from outside. It was a whole assortment of different sounds – a baby crying, someone shouting, and the quiet thud of music.

I slowly walked over to the house. Next to the door was a line of various buzzers with names pasted on them, and I realized stupidly that I didn't even know Alice's last name. Feeling reckless, I just pressed the third one down – Carter. I don't know why, it just felt right.

The booming voice that answered confirmed that it wasn't.

"Yes? Who is it?"

"Sorry, I'm here for Alice? I pressed the wrong number."

There was a silence. Then the voice came back. Softer now.

"The sad girl? In the flat with the babies?"

Sad girl? That didn't quite sound right. I thought back to the day that I saw Alice in the waiting room with her mum. There *had* been young kids with her.

"Yeah," I answered. "I'm sorry. I forgot which number she lives at. I'm a friend from school."

There was another pause, like the voice was considering the information.

"Try number four," he said at last.

I thanked him, even though it was pretty clear he had already gone. Then, before I could change my mind, I stabbed my finger at the fourth button down.

Nothing.

I stood there for a bit, wondering if I should try again. But would that seem rude? What if the man had given me the wrong number, or what if they weren't in?

I was just about to walk away when the speaker crackled and a female voice spoke. In the background I could hear the baby crying again.

"Who is it?"

The voice sounded spiky. Definitely not friendly. I coughed, feeling uneasy now. Maybe this wasn't such a good idea.

"I'm here to see Alice. It's Alfie?"

There was silence again, and I cast my gaze up towards the windows, wondering which one was theirs. All the curtains were tightly drawn – it was as if the house was shut off to the rest of the world.

Finally, the speaker crackled again.

"Come up. We're on the second floor, number four. Make sure you wipe your feet."

The buzzer went off, and, slightly confused, I pulled open the heavy front door.

It was strangely lit inside, quite dark and dreary. I guessed that was because all the doors were closed. The hall, which I imagined was once quite grand and posh, was stripped of light and colour. Even the carpets had been taken up. I could smell dampness and dust. I climbed the wooden stairs up to the second floor. The whole house seemed alive, as if each room had a heartbeat: the movement of people, the rise and fall of voices. It was strange thinking about all these different people tucked away in different areas of the house. There was something quite lonely about it.

Number four was on the left, with a small brass number plate pinned to the door. Outside was a rusty-looking scooter and a line of welly boots. I walked over and rapped on the door cautiously. It was opened quickly, but only by about an inch so that a face could peer round. I could just about make out a blue eye and a smudge of a cheek.

"Let me see you. Are you alone?"

I moved more into her line of sight. "I'm alone. It's just me."

The door opened a little further. I could now see her properly – the woman who I assumed was Alice's mum. She was dressed casually, in baggy jeans and a huge cream jumper. Her dark hair was gathered up into a rough bun. She looked a little like Alice, just chubbier, with greyer looking skin. I could see shadows under her eyes and deep frown lines etched into her forehead. On her hip sat a little baby dressed in a pink Babygro.

"Alfie?" she repeated, looking me up and down. "And you're a friend of Alice's?"

I shifted a little on the spot. "I guess you could say that."

She sniffed. "Then you better come in."

So I did. Walking through the doorway, I'd expected to find myself in a hallway, but instead I walked straight into a room. And that was all there was. One room: a double bed on one side, a pull-out bed on another side and a cot under the window. Apart from a small chest of drawers and a tatty-looking wardrobe, the room was kind of bare.

On the bed sat a little boy, looking at a comic. I guessed he was around five or six years old. He peered up at me as soon I walked in. He was just like Alice with the same sulky mouth and large, bright eyes.

There was no sign of Alice at all.

Her mum caught me staring. "That's Henry," she said. "Say hello, Henry. This is Alfie, one of Alice's friends."

Henry looked at me, wide eyed. "Do you like football? I do." He held up his comic. It was a football one, the same one I used to buy.

I shrugged. "Yeah, I do."

Henry grinned. "Will you play with me?"

"Henry!" Alice's mum glared at him and then turned

back to me. "Sorry, he gets so bored being cooped up in this place. I struggle to take him out without Alice here."

"Where *is* Alice?" I asked.

Her mum looked down, and I was suddenly aware of how young she seemed to be. She was a lot younger than my mum had been. She almost looked like she could be in sixth form.

"I don't know," she said finally. "I never know. I guess I was hoping you could help with that."

And then she burst into tears.

They stood by the seafront. It was winter, and so cold that the air pinched at his skin and made his eyes all watery. They were alone. Completely alone, in fact – there was no one else for miles around them. Just them, the roaring grey sea and a few hungry-looking gulls.

She was wrapped up tight in a large winter coat. It totally swamped her. Her hands, so white and so thin, clasped the black railings. Her fingernails were unpainted now. Most of her was white and without colour. He turned to his mum and tried not to cry as she looked back at him. He could see the sickness so clearly now. It was there in the shadows on her skin, the dryness of her lips and the sadness in her eyes.

She was a living ghost. He was losing her.

Gently she began to sing under her breath:

"She died of a fever,

And no one could save her,
And that was the end of sweet Molly Malone.
But her ghost wheels her barrow,
Through streets broad and narrow,
Crying, 'Cockles and mussels, alive, alive, oh!'"

The words stung his ears. He couldn't bear it and he turned away from her – from her voice, from the sweetly sung words that now seemed too cruel.

As he staggered away, the words played again and again in his tired mind.

"No one could save her."

No one.

Chapter Fifteen

It's kind of awkward when someone you don't know, especially an adult, cries in front of you. I've never been any good with that sort of stuff and I found myself just standing there, not knowing what to say, wishing I had a tissue or something to offer her. Was that something people even did?

"Are you OK?" I ended up saying instead, pretty lamely.

Alice's mum peered back at me with red-rimmed eyes. She was sitting on the edge of the bed, slowly rocking the baby back and forth. I guessed the movement was soothing them both a bit. I noticed that a bubble of snot was forming on the end of her nose and I looked away quickly, embarrassed.

Why did I come here? What was I thinking?

"I'm sorry," she said finally. She swept the back of her hand over her nose. It was a bit gross but at least that snot was gone. "I shouldn't have got upset like that. I'm just tired, that's all."

I nodded. Tiredness was one thing I did understand.

"I don't sleep much either," I said.

Her eyes widened slightly. "It's awful, isn't it? The worst thing. My mind just doesn't turn off – and then one of these wakes up. . ." She nods towards the baby. "I dunno. . . I just feel like a zombie at the moment."

"It must be hard, with kids and that," I said.

She sighed. "Yeah. It's really hard."

The silence returned. She was rocking the baby again and muttering softly in his ear. Henry was just staring at me, obviously a bit confused by it all. He wasn't the only one. I smiled at him and he looked away again.

"I just wanted Alice," I said finally.

That sounded wrong. I didn't exactly want her. I wanted to be in her company, that was all. At least, I thought I did.

"She was shouting," Henry said suddenly, his little

eyes bright. "She said bad words at Mummy and ran away. She made the door slam."

I saw Alice's mum's cheeks redden. "Henry! She *was* angry. I guess I thought you might know where she'd gone, being her friend?"

I felt bad. I wished I could help more. "No, sorry – I don't really know. . ."

She slumped back a little. "We haven't been here long, you probably know that. And Alice is struggling with the move. She's never been very good with change."

"We had to move away because my daddy was nasty," Henry said.

"That's enough, Henry," said Alice's mum, resting a hand on his leg. "Alice's friend doesn't need to know all about that."

It was true, I didn't need to know, but I wanted to know. Alice had kept everything so quiet; I didn't really know anything about her. I realized that I really wanted to.

"Alice didn't want to leave London, that's all," she said, her eyes fixed on me. "It's hardly glamorous here, I know, but it's a new start and hopefully we'll have a flat of our own soon."

I nodded again, not really knowing what to say.

This was a tiny room, cluttered, damp and dimly lit. I could see why Alice wanted to be outside all the time. I'd be the same.

"She just stormed out then?" I said finally.

Her mum nodded. "Yeah. She's in trouble at school again... That girl, I just don't know why she can't keep her nose clean for five minutes." She paused. "Hang on, they said she was with another student. Was that you?"

My cheeks reddened. "Yeah."

What was the point of lying? I was rubbish at it anyway.

Her face hardened. "Listen – Alfie, wasn't it? I'll be honest. It's people like you she needs to stay away from. Bad influences. Alice has a chance to turn her life around, not be dragged back down."

Dragged down? Was she for real? I snorted. I couldn't help myself.

"I'm not dragging Alice down," I said, aware of the sudden loudness of my voice. "I was trying to help her."

Alice's mum shifted on the bed. I noticed she was shaking a bit. Her arms gripped the baby a little tighter.

"I'm sorry, Alfie – I shouldn't have said that."

Her voice was so small, like she had lost all of her power.

"Don't worry," I said calmly, making my way back towards the door. "I'll find Alice for you. I'll tell her to come home." I paused. "But you have to believe me, I'm not dragging her down. She seems to be doing that all by herself."

He didn't want to go, not at first. It all seemed so wrong. All of it. Too fast and out of control — but it was Granddad who persuaded him.

"She wants to see you, Alfie. I know you're scared, but try to do this. She's still your mum."

They both stood in the dining room, looking out at the garden. Winter had come and a deep frost had settled on the branches and leaves. The entire scene looked different, as if it had been caught under an icy spell.

The sunflower was long gone, of course. Back in the earth, ready to spring up again when the weather improved. But he missed it. He wanted to see the bright yellow petals, the silly nodding head. He wanted their reassurance.

Granddad's hand rested on his shoulder.

"C'mon, son. Your dad is waiting in the car."

Dad. Outside. Always away from them. He'd barely seen him recently. He'd been at work or visiting Mum at that place, but either way he was like a stranger now. A shadow in his life.

They walked to the car together. He saw Dad sitting in the front, staring straight ahead, not even looking up to acknowledge him. Fine. He didn't want to talk anyway. There were no words left to say. He folded himself into the back seat and leant up against the window, staring out. Dad and Granddad talked on the way, but he didn't listen. He wasn't interested in any of it.

The hospice was only a five-minute drive away. Too short. When they pulled up, he felt his stomach dive. His legs were fixed to the seat.

He couldn't move.

He couldn't do this.

This was her last place – this was where she had come to die.

She was never coming back.

Granddad turned in his seat. "It's OK," he said, "take your time."

But Dad had already unbuckled his seatbelt. He sighed loudly, ran a hand over his hair. "Stop making a drama out of this," he hissed, opening the door. "You need to do this for her."

Then he slammed the door so hard behind him that it shook the car.

He watched his dad walk towards to hospice door, not turning, not looking back. He was going in there with or without him.

He didn't care.

"He's not coping well," Granddad said softly. "This isn't about you."

But he knew it was all about him. He was letting them down. He wasn't strong enough.

But he still couldn't move.

He remained in that seat. Frozen.

Chapter Sixteen

Somehow I knew she'd be there, even though she had no right to be. My mum's and my favourite place. It was like she was stealing it from us. She was leant up against the railings, her head tipped slightly forward so that the wind had hold of her hair. It was whipping around all over the place, but she didn't seem to mind. She was barely moving.

"Alice?" I said, approaching her carefully, as if she was a small wild animal that could scare and run away.

She turned her head a little, and I could make out her red cheek, the curl of her smile and her eye half closed against the wind.

"What are you doing here?" she asked.

"Looking for you."

I pulled myself up next to her and took in a lungful of sea air. Mum always used to say that it could clear your head, sweep all the badness away.

"Looking for me. . .?" Alice let the statement hang for a moment. "Interesting."

"Why interesting?"

"I just wonder why, that's all." She turned her head away again. "Is there something you want?"

I wasn't sure how to answer that. Had I wanted something? I guess I'd wanted her company, but that sounded completely weird and not something that I wanted to admit.

"I went to your house," I said instead. "Your mum didn't know where you were."

Alice stepped off the railings and turned fully to look at me, one hand pushing the hair away from her face. The smile had gone now. She looked angry.

"You went to my house? Why did you do that?"

"I dunno. I just thought. . ." I realized too late that I didn't know what I'd thought. Why *had* I gone to her house? "I dunno. . ." I repeated pointlessly.

"I didn't want you going to my house," she snapped. I'd seen her angry before – seen her fly off the handle – but this was something different.

"Why?" I said. "Why is it such a big deal?"

"It doesn't matter," she said, shaking her head. "Just go now, please. I'm here because I want some time on my own."

"Are you being serious? You seemed pleased to see me when I first came over – what changed?"

Her head whipped back towards the sea, her arms crossed against her body. She obviously hadn't wanted me to go to her house. The more I thought on it the more I realized that she'd purposefully kept me away from there before. I shouldn't have knocked for her like I did. I should have read the signs.

"Look – I'm sorry I did the wrong thing by going to your house. I figured you'd be there. I was bored and – I just – I just thought you might want to hang out..."

She still wouldn't look at me, but I could tell she was listening.

"Your mum was dead friendly," I carried on, "and I wasn't even there long..." I sighed, feeling stupid and awkward. "She seemed really upset. She was worried about you. She didn't know where you were."

"My *mum* is none of your business," Alice snapped, still facing the sea. Still not looking at me.

"I just felt a bit sorry for her," I said carefully.

"Sorry for her!" Alice's words were like fireworks streaking across the sky. "You know nothing about her. Yeah, she worries about me when it suits her."

I shook my head. "I'm sorry, Alice. I don't know what the deal is with you two."

She half laughed. "All you need to know is that Mum messes everything up. We've spent *years* going from place to place because she has had one failed relationship after another. Did you know that the last guy she was with beat her up so badly I had to take her to hospital in a taxi myself? One I couldn't even pay for? And now she spends every day worrying that he'll find us. Yeah, she worries about me too, but I can't bear to be there with her. I hate my life. I detest it. I hate what we've become. And I can't say I'm too bothered about going to school. We'll only move again soon anyway when she gets scared, so what's the point?"

"I'm sorry," I said, dropping my gaze. "I really am. I didn't know."

"You didn't ask! I guess you just thought I was some waster. You make assumptions like they all do. You're too wrapped in your own problems to see that you're not the only one with a far-from-perfect life."

I couldn't speak. I didn't know what to say. She was right, of course. I *hadn't* bothered to think about what was going on her life, or anyone else's. I'd just told myself that she was messed up and that was all there was to it. I'd been so completely absorbed in my own stuff. I hadn't bothered to even ask her about hers.

"I'm sorry," she said finally. "I know your mum died recently. That's obviously awful. But you walk around like you've given up on everything. I don't get it. I don't see how that helps anything."

"You don't understand. . ."

She shrugged. "No, maybe I don't. But that's what's different about us. I have to get on, I have to keep going. I can't let everything swallow me up and make me feel even worse than I already do."

"But does running away from stuff all the time help?" I asked, and I wasn't being sarcastic, I actually wanted to know. "Surely you're being a bit like her? Like your mum?"

I put my hand gently on her shoulder. She flinched, but she didn't whack it away.

"I'm your mate, Alice," I said. And for the first time I realized that it was true. She was messed up – and, yeah, so was I – but we *had* been there for each other, in a way. So she *was* my mate. And I cared about her.

Alice didn't say anything, but I felt her shoulder slump a little beneath my hand.

"I know I've been caught up in my own head, but I *am* here for you," I said quietly, and she slowly turned around. I could see tears in those huge fiery eyes of hers, see the lines they'd made down her face.

"Really?" she said.

"Yeah, really."

She tipped her head so that it was resting against my hand. "Thank you," she whispered.

We moved down on to the beach and sat on the pebbles. There was this good feeling between us. It was kind of difficult to explain, but I could tell that Alice was acting differently – calmer somehow, maybe more sad. Her normal confident act seemed to have been washed away, exposing all of the emotion that had been covered up before. Sitting next to me deep in thought, she rocked slowly against the breeze with her arms locked around her knees.

"Do you want my jumper?" I asked.

I remembered how I'd judged her for only wearing a thin jacket when we first met. Why had I been such an idiot? If I'd known that she was living out of a suitcase – sharing one room with her whole family – I might not have been so quick to judge. Or would I? It had been so easy to make a judgement about her when I didn't know everything she was up against.

She shook her head. "I'm OK."

"Do you want something to eat?"

She shook her head again.

"Something to drink?"

She turned towards me, her eyes glinting. "Stop fussing, Alfie. I'm fine."

We sat quietly for a while and then Alice turned to me again.

"Did you mean what you said earlier? About being my mate?"

I nodded. Yeah. Yeah, I did.

She pushed her hair away from her face.

"Fancy spending some time with me tomorrow? I mean I'll probably have to help with the kids in the morning, but maybe we could meet up later?" She screwed up her face. "Unless you've got something more exciting lined up?"

Exciting? Seriously? She was having a laugh. Of course before my weekends would have been packed with training, matches, the occasional tournaments.

But now they were just long, empty voids.

Time that needed to be filled.

"That sounds good," I said.

It was nice to see her smile back at me.

He was trying to act like everything was still the same.

Home, school, friends. If he acted like nothing had changed, then perhaps it would be OK. Maybe life would stay the same. His dad would be relaxed and happy. His mum would come out of that awful hospice and return home. He'd see her sitting in the garden, singing softly under her breath.

And they would be normal again. Whatever normal was.

He wouldn't have to keep thinking about this stuff. He wouldn't have to deal with the awful, gut-pulling thoughts that made his body heavy, made his head hurt. He couldn't let those thoughts take over. He was scared that if he did, everything would stop.

If he could just act normal. If he pasted a smile on his face and carried on, it would be fine. But Dad was barely ever at home, and when he was he might as well not have been. He didn't want to talk. He didn't want to be bothered. So they both did their own thing. They both ignored each other. They both hoped that this horrible problem would just disappear.

He walked to school, not hearing Ben calling him, being surprised when the boy ran up beside him and tugged his arm. They had been mates once, ages ago, until they suddenly weren't any more. He looked at the spiked hair and bright eyes. What did he want?

"Hey!" Ben said. "You're late for school. That's not like you."

He half nodded. It was true. The walk seemed to take longer these days. Getting out of bed was harder. Some mornings he just lay there, wide awake, wondering if he could actually face the day. Even with the light streaming in through his window, the room seemed cloaked in darkness. He used to get up and out early – to play football with the others on the astro pitch. But now he could barely move.

"I'm not feeling too good," he said to Ben, who didn't say anything for a while. Then suddenly a stream of words burst from Ben's lips.

"Mate, I heard about your mum. She's sick, right? I'm so sorry. She's cool. I remember how she used to make us ice lollies in the summer. I didn't know whether to say anything. I know no one else is saying anything – but, I dunno. . . I just wanted to, you know. . ."

He stared back at Ben, not used to hearing someone actually talk about it. Everyone else had been so quiet.

"Anyway. . ." Ben continued, " I just wanted to say it's totally rubbish that this is happening."

He nodded. "Yeah, it is."

Ben sighed. "I know you hang out with Cole and that lot, but if you ever want to. . . Well, I'm here for you?"

He thought about his football mates. The loud jokes, the ribbing, the constant competing. He doubted if any of them either knew or cared what he was going through at moment. They didn't feel like proper mates any more.

"Thanks, mate. I appreciate that."

Ben smiled at him. "There are people here for you, Alfie. Don't forget that."

The problem was, he did forget.

Chapter Seventeen

I got back home just after seven and was starving. Dad was out, which wasn't too surprising. He'd probably gone to the pub, or round to his mate Brian's house. He obviously liked being anywhere that wasn't here. I felt a stab of sadness. Was this ever going to change?

I grabbed some food from the kitchen and saw that Dad had left stew in the slow cooker.

Won't be late too home. Make sure you eat. We need to talk later, said the note lying next to it.

I left the brown muck to congeal and got some bread and cheese instead, suddenly not feeling all that hungry. I looked into the living room as I walked past. We barely ever went in there now, with me basically living in my bedroom and Dad in his, so it usually stayed pretty much untouched. I could see that it obviously hadn't been cleaned for ages. There was dust on everything, and plenty of cobwebs hanging from the ceiling. It smelled weirdly musty too, like someone needed to crack open a window. When Mum was alive she cleaned and polished all the time. She'd hate to see it like this.

My eyes fell to the photos on the mantelpiece. Mum and Dad's wedding day. They looked so happy. Her in a huge white dress, with hair all big and fluffy, her eyes lit up with happiness. And Dad. Dad looked so different. Softer. His eyes are fixed on Mum – it's as if he can't see anything but her.

There's another photo next to it, one of all three of us. I remember it being taken – but I was pretty young, and Mum hired some professional photographer who got us posing in the garden. Dad kept moaning about how long it was taking and Mum kept giggling and hitting him for being grumpy. He's crouching behind us both and laughing, which is pretty rare to see. Mum looks beautiful. Her hair is long and shiny, her arms wrapped around my middle, like she'd never let go.

I think she was diagnosed for the first time a few weeks after the photo was taken.

This photo was taken when everything was good. When we were happy.

I wished I could go back. I'd tell the old me to hold on to that moment. To enjoy it while it lasted. Because it wouldn't last.

Nothing did.

I must've dozed off. I woke up to my phone buzzing next to me, and for a few seconds I wondered where I was. It took a while for me to recognize the room in the semi-darkness. I had fallen asleep on the sofa.

I stared at the shadowed shapes around me, still half-asleep. It was like parts of my old life were becoming less and less familiar. They were rooted firmly in the past and growing more and more distant by the day. I shifted on the seat, feeling a crick in my neck where I'd obviously slept in an awkward position. I rubbed at my sore point, feeling the tightened muscle pushing under my skin. Feeling the tension there.

I reached for my phone, thinking maybe it was Dad making contact (yeah, right) or Alice checking about tomorrow. I scanned the message, feeling a jolt of surprise. It wasn't Alice. It wasn't even Dad. It was Cole.

Hey – it's been too long. Me and the lads are
going over the field tomorrow morning. Fancy
a game?

I stared at the words, not sure how they were
making me feel. This wasn't like Cole. Since Mum
had died he'd been really weird with me. I guess he
couldn't handle what had happened. Cole wasn't one
for talking about feelings, I knew that. But even so,
he hadn't texted me for months – he'd just avoided
me like I had some kind of disease. So this felt new.

My finger hovered over the screen. I hadn't played
football for so long, and even thinking about it felt
wrong now. Could I even play any more? The last
time had been that day. That awful, awful day when
Mum...

... when Mum died.

But this was different, I guess. This was just a
kick around.

My stomach twisted. I missed it. I did *really* miss
it.

But...

It wasn't the same now.

I stared at the screen for a bit longer and finally
punched out my reply.

Sorry mate. I'm not free.

His reply was swift. Maybe he was waiting for it. I bet he was expecting it.

Never mind – another time maybe. Just text me.

I nodded to myself.

Yeah.

Maybe. . .

I looked back to the photo of Mum, Dad and me, and felt the pressure building up behind my eyes. I swallowed once. Twice. And blinked hard. I wasn't going to break down. Not today.

I got up quickly and walked over to the photo. I couldn't stand to look at our stupid, beaming faces any longer. The picture was mocking me. Having to look at how happy we used to be, knowing that we could never feel that way again, that was cruel and unfair. I flung my arm across the mantelpiece, knocking everything to the ground, hearing it crash and crack. As I stepped back, I felt one of the frames underneath my foot and booted it across the room.

I needed it gone. All of it.

I couldn't bear to remember how good things used to be.

How it could never be that way again.

*

Dad didn't come home till after eleven and by that time I was back in my room. He didn't even attempt to be quiet – he slammed the front door, stomped up the stairs, made plenty of noise in the bathroom.

Then he rapped on my door. "Alfie? Are you awake?"

There was no point pretending otherwise. Dad knew that I struggled to sleep now. I walked over to the door and opened it. Then I sat back down on my bed.

He followed me in. He looked scruffy. His T-shirt was un-ironed and tucked half in and half out of his jeans, which seemed to be hanging strangely on him. Had he lost weight? He rubbed his head across his shaven scalp. I could smell beer on him.

"You shouldn't have walked out earlier. I didn't even know where you'd gone."

I dipped my head. "I'm sorry, Dad. I just needed to get out."

"I can't have you – I can't have you doing stuff like this..." His words were slurred, like they were too big for his mouth. Dad didn't drink often, so it was really weird seeing him like this. He was wobbling a bit and blinking hard at me. His hand reached out to the end of the bed so he could balance himself.

"I'm sorry," I said again. And I meant it. I really did.

He was shaking his head. "It's hard... So hard. You don't know. You don't know what it's like. I'm trying, son. I'm really trying..." His words caught in his throat and I looked up at him. I could see tears in his bloodshot eyes.

"It's OK, Dad."

"No... No. It's not OK. I can't be her. I can't!" His hand slammed on the bed, making it shake. His voice was louder now and unsteady. "I can't be your mum. I wish, I wish so much...

"Dad..."

He stared at me, tears streaming down his face. He looked so lost, so broken. It made me feel like my insides were being torn up. I'd never seen him like this. What was I supposed to do?

"I can't do this," he said. "I can't do this without her..."

I got up and went towards him. I don't know what I was going to do. Hug him? Tell him I felt the same? I don't know. But I needed to do something.

I gently reached out and touched his arm.

Dad hesitated. His glassy eyes fixed on mine, then he peered down at my hand. I realized that I was trembling.

"I miss her too," I whispered.

I could feel his arm vibrate. He was shaking, his throat making gasping, gulpy sounds as he tried to force back the sobs.

"Dad?" I said. "Dad, are you...?"

He lifted his head up. His eyes were full. Tears spilt out clumsily on to his cheeks, down around his mouth. He swallowed and gasped.

"Oh, Alfie," he whispered. "Oh, God. I miss her too much."

His hand grabbed my head and pulled it towards his chest. I could hear his heart pounding, feel every vibration of his sobs.

"It's OK, Dad," I said.

Just standing there, pressed up against his warm, beating body. I don't know why. It just helped. I closed my eyes.

He's still here.

My dad.

He's here.

It was the first time I'd seen him cry in front of me.

It was like he would never stop.

He was here. This time he was going to do this. He was going to go inside.

The knot in his stomach rested heavily inside him, but he refused to acknowledge it. It was only feelings. Stupid feelings and fear. This was his mum – his mum! He couldn't keep running away.

The hospice was brighter than he imagined, and it smelt fresh and clean. Not like the hospital smell that he was expecting. Not clinical or cold, but warm and friendly. It was calm here. Peaceful.

A nurse had greeted him and Granddad when they came through the entrance and asked if they wanted a drink. She smiled down at him brightly, like she was genuinely pleased that he was there.

"You're Alfie, aren't you? Your mum will be so happy you're here – she talks so much about you."

He tried to smile back. He knew it wasn't a true smile – it was the one he painted on to show everyone that he was all right.

Even though he wasn't. He wasn't at all.

He didn't want to see her.

He bit down hard on his lip. He couldn't think like that. His dad had been firm – almost angry with him for refusing before. He had to stop being selfish. He had to put her first.

They walked through the large airy hall, past a grand piano and several comfy-looking sofas.

"You're welcome to come and sit out here, any time," The nurse told him. She grinned again. "My name's Charlotte. I'm with your mum a lot. She's a lovely lady."

He nodded, feeling proud, but he couldn't say anything. The knot in his stomach was tightening. It felt like his stomach would turn in on itself if the knot got any tighter.

He couldn't do this.

But his feet continued to move him forward, towards her room. Charlotte was talking lightly to his dad and his dad was answering politely back, and all the time all he wanted to do was shout at both of them:

Shut up! Shut up! Shut up!

He sucked in air, drove his hands into his pockets and tried to close off that part of his brain. If he just concentrated on this moment – on this second – he could get through. He put one foot in front of the other.

Now he had his hand on the door.

Now he was pushing it open.

Now he was stepping into the room.

Now he was looking at Mum.

Mum. . .

He felt himself sag as relief and sadness flooded through him. It made him feel dizzy and sick at the same time. She was sitting up in bed, smiling at him. She looked happy. Her eyes were bright and shiny, and her lips were drawn up into a wide smile.

But he could see the difference in her. The loose skin around her neck, her thin arms, the greyness around her eyes.

She was fading.

But in that moment she still sparkled.

She was still Mum.

Chapter Eighteen

Saturdays are normally rubbish. I hate weekends. They are worse than school days now – long, drawn-out hours that used to fly by. Saturday morning training, afternoons in town or down the park with the lads. Sunday would always be a game and then it would be family time. A walk, a pub lunch, an afternoon on the beach.

Then our happy little set-up was destroyed. Maybe we had it too good. Maybe we had to be taught a lesson. Not once, but twice. Give Mum cancer to start with and then let her beat it. Give us years of thinking everything was going to be fine, and then serve us the sucker punch, the killer blow. Hit her with it again. But this time, put the cancer really deep inside her. Sink it into her bones, bury it in her liver. See how she deals with that. See what happens to the happy little family then, when the one thing that holds them together is gone.

Well, I'll tell you what happened: the happy little family snapped.

And it couldn't be fixed, because we didn't have the tools to fix it. We were just two ends of a destroyed chain, dangling, not knowing what to do.

We were lost.

Ben messaged me while I was eating my breakfast, asking me if I fancied going into town with him and a few of his mates. I guessed it was that group from school. They seemed all right, but I just couldn't see myself fitting in with them – and the thought of hanging around like some sad cling-on was worse than being alone. So I said no. But I was glad he asked.

Dad was barely talking. He probably had a hangover. He sat opposite me, drinking his tea and reading his phone. I could tell he was tried. His eyes were hooded and his face was pale. He looked like he hadn't slept for months.

"I'm sorry about last night," he said softly, rubbing

his face. "I had too much to drink with the lads and, you know. . . I didn't mean to get all. . ."

His voice drifted off.

I sat back, held his gaze. "It was OK, Dad. Honestly."

We actually held eye contact. I saw something flicker behind his eyes. Something that told me that he understood what I was saying.

It was fine, Dad. You cried. So what?

I'm so glad you did.

I needed you to do that.

I pushed my empty plate to one side. "I might go out," I said. "If that's OK?"

"I guess. . ." He looked up at me, half smiled. "What are you going to be doing?"

"I dunno. I was going to meet up with Alice, but that's later. I might just go for a walk or something."

He nodded. "Sounds nice. But I was thinking, maybe. . ." He coughed, like he was nervous or something. "Maybe we could do something together first?"

His eyes met mine. They were softer now. Calmer. There was something so familiar, so comforting in the way he was looking at me that it almost made me want to sob.

This was my dad. My old dad.

"Like what?" I asked

"We could go to a game." He paused, giving me time to think about the idea. "Town are playing at home today; they have an early kick-off. I was going to go along. It's been a while. Too long, in fact. I wondered if you fancied it."

I frowned. I hadn't seen our local team play for ages, but Dad and me used to wander up to their grounds sometimes, especially if I didn't have a game myself. I used to like those cold afternoons spent on the sidelines, clutching a hot chocolate and cheering for our team to win. Even though most of the time they didn't.

We hadn't done this since Mum had died.

"I dunno. . ."

The feeling of unease was still gnawing inside of me. I couldn't pretend to be that person any more. So much had changed.

Dad reached forward and gently tapped my hand.

"C'mon, son, just one game. What harm can it do?" He grinned. "You never know, you might enjoy it."

We stood where we always used to, a few rows back near the halfway line. Dad liked to be close to the action, even though it meant risking a ball in the face at any point during the game. It was busier than usual and there were already quite a few people in the seats around us. I also noticed that the stands and both ends were pretty much full.

"Big cup game today," Dad said. "They need to win this one to stay in."

I nodded, like I already knew, but of course I didn't – and knowing that made my insides ache. I hadn't been following this stuff for the past few months and it suddenly felt like I'd been left behind and the rest of the world had just carried on without me.

We knew most people there, and Dad was chatting to a few of the blokes sitting near to us. He nudged me, nodding his head in my direction.

"This is my son, Alfie," he told the man sitting closest. He was about Dad's age, skinny with a mess of ginger hair. He had a kid next him, who looked younger than me and wasn't even a little bit interested in us – was too busy looking at his phone.

The man grinned, offered us both his hand. "I'm Tony. This is my boy, Max."

Max looked up – kind of half smiled at us and then went back to his phone. He was skinny like his dad with the same bright ginger hair. I recognized him from somewhere.

"First game we've been to in a while. . ." Dad was saying. "It's good to be back."

Tony snorted, rubbing his gloved hands together. "I wouldn't get too excited, not the way these lads have been playing lately. It's been pitiful. My Max could give them a run for their money."

Max sighed and rolled his eyes. Suddenly I remembered where I'd seen him before.

"You play for Heathfield!" I said quickly, before I could stop myself.

Max looked up. It was like he saw me for the first time. His eyes widened. "Oh my God – you're from the team we played last season. Cookbridge? Man, I couldn't believe you guys. You smashed us."

I smiled – I couldn't help myself. "Nah. It was a tough game."

He laughed. "Yeah, right. You were all over us. Especially you. You just make it look easy."

My cheeks burned. "Cheers – but I'm not that good."

Not any more anyway. . .

"Aren't you playing at the moment?" he asked.

I shrugged. "No." I paused for a second. "I'm injured."

"Ah! Me too!" He sighed. "My hamstring is playing up, what about you?"

"My knee," I said. It was the first thing that came to me.

"You're a great player, you know," he said finally. "Our coach was laying into us for the whole of that game. Telling us that we needed to mark you. You were impossible to catch."

"Thanks."

Max leant closer towards me. "Didn't something happen in our game though? Between you and your mate? You—"

"No," I said firmly, interrupting him. "It was nothing. I had to come off because I was injured. That's all."

The lies flowed so easily.

Dad leant in. I could see the beam creeping across his face. "Alfie could make it. He's been told he has real potential." He turned to Tony. "He had trials lined up, you know? For *two* major clubs. We just had to turn them down."

Tony seemed impressed. I could feel myself squirm. "Really? So why aren't you at an academy already?"

Dad patted my arm. "He could've been. But he wanted to wait. Plus there was lots of stuff going on at home, you know? The timing wasn't right. It would've been a lot of pressure."

Seriously? This wasn't like Dad to be talking so openly. I looked at him, surprised, but he smiled back at me weakly.

"I can't wait for him to start playing again," he said, his eyes fixed on mine. "I think it'll help both of us."

Something inside of me sparked.

He wants me to play again.

I dipped my head, swallowed hard. What about me? What did I want?

"I bet you miss it," Max said to me, like he could read my mind. "You're so good. It must feel so natural for you."

"I've been playing most of my life," I muttered.

And yes, I did miss it. I really did.

The noise was building in the ground now. The game was starting. The whistle blew. Something inside me fired up. A warmth, an excitement that I thought I'd buried away. The crowd roared. My blood was rushing.

I closed my eyes. I remembered.

I remembered how I felt when the crowd roared for me.

Soon I was on my feet with the rest of them.

Cheering. Chanting. Becoming part of it all again.

"C'mon!"

"C'MON!"

After the match, Dad was definitely in a brighter mood, and I suppose I was too. It helped that we'd won. We'd both been swept up into the roaring swell of the crowd. There was no way you could feel miserable when hundreds of people around you were so excited.

"*Fantastic* game," Dad said, as we swung out of the turnstiles and moved through the crowds. "That's the best I've seen them play for ages."

"They were good, they totally deserved it," I agreed. It had been fast action from start to finish – amazing runs from the wingers, powerful control from the front and a solid defence. There really wasn't much to criticize. They were unlucky not to score more than the three that they did.

"So you knew that lad? Max?" Dad said casually.

I nodded. "Yeah. I played against him a few times. . ." I paused. "He was at my last game."

Dad was silent for a moment. "Oh. I see."

We kept walking, and it was a while before Dad spoke again. "That game. You shouldn't think too much on it. I know you and Cole had that run in, but it was a difficult time. Your mum and everything."

A run in? That was putting it mildly.

"He was an idiot," I muttered.

"He just doesn't get it. It's hard for. . ." Dad rubbed a hand across his stubble. "It's hard for some of us to talk about things like that."

"He was winding me up. On purpose."

"That's what lads do sometimes."

I frowned. "It was more than that. You don't get it."

We carried on walking. I was starting to feel restless again. I hated thinking back, re-running that last game of the season. The match that finished things for me. If I had played better it might've been OK. If Cole hadn't started gobbing off, maybe things could've been different.

If I had been with Mum instead. . .

Because that was it really. The guilt that I had chosen to play over being with her. How could I ever act the same again?

My pace slowed. I felt like I was dragging my feet

now, really struggling to keep up with Dad's long strides. He noticed and slowed down.

"You OK?"

"I'm fine."

Dad placed a hand on my shoulder. "Do you know what? I really enjoyed today. It was good just being together, us two. I haven't done enough of this with you."

I didn't answer.

"Alfie – I know it's been difficult for both of us. But I'm trying – I'm trying to get things back to normal. . ." His voice shook a little. "To some kind of normal, anyway."

He wanted us to be normal, but I didn't even know if that was possible. How could I ever feel normal again when part of me – part of us – was missing for ever?

I looked up at him – really looked. Tried to see him as someone I didn't know, a total stranger. His face was serious, his eyes were soft and kind but lined with shadows. His mouth drawn tight, as if he was fighting back more words. I wanted him to be able to feel happiness again. I wanted him to know that it was going to be OK, because suddenly I realized that he was scared too. He was scared that we were falling apart.

"It's all right, Dad," I said. "It'll be all right."

He squeezed my shoulder and nodded.

We started walking again, and I tried to keep to his pace. I tried to keep my head up high and my face calm. I tried not to think too much.

"You could think about playing again," he said. "It might be good for you."

Could I play again? Watching the game *had* reminded me that there was something else missing from my life. Something that I might be able to get back. But would it ever be the same?

Dad smiled. "One step at a time. Maybe you could just go to a training session. I know Cookbridge would love to see you back."

My skin prickled at the thought. Being back with the lads. Joking around with Cole again. Could that be possible?

"Maybe," I said.

"Just think about it, son. Please."

We were almost home. Dad slowed down and half turned, away from me this time, as if he was looking across the street at someone. "I think we can do this, Alfie. Both of us. We can help each other."

I sucked in air. I tried to stop the shake in my voice. "Yeah. I do too."

He knew something was different before he had even stepped into the room. It was as if the energy had shifted somehow – the air felt heavier, the space around him seemed tighter, the noises of the hospice were louder. He knew that he wasn't going to like what he saw.

He hesitated outside the door, his stupid legs once again refusing to move, his hands too clammy against the handle.

His dad came up behind him and gently eased him through the door. Charlotte was there again, standing just inside. Waiting for them both. When he stepped inside, his eyes went immediately to the bed, and he had to force back a groan. He shoved his hands in his pockets, gripped the material inside. He wanted to look away, but he couldn't, he just couldn't. His eyes were locked on the figure in the bed.

In just a week, she had been replaced by a skeleton.

There were tubes in her nose helping her to breathe. Her eyes were closed. She wasn't wearing a wig or a headscarf, and he could see her thinning hair, the pink of her scalp. Her tiny, bone-like hands rested on the sheets that covered her.

But it was her face that made him want to cry. Her protruding cheek bones. Her skin resting on the bones.

His mum. His poor, poor mum.

She looked so ill.

Dad walked over. Took one of her tiny, brittle hands in his own. It looked like it would snap, he thought. He couldn't look, and his eyes dropped to the floor.

"Babe," Dad was saying, his voice barely there. "My poor baby."

He noticed a hand on his shoulder. Charlotte.

"Sit with her, Alfie. It's OK," she whispered in his ear

He nodded and slowly walked over to the other side of the bed, sitting down on the chair there. He could see Mum was wearing her favourite grey pyjamas, the really soft, expensive ones that Dad had bought her last Christmas. She always looked so cosy in them. She still did.

He reached forward and took her other hand. It was thin, but it was warm and soft. Her fingers wiggled in his grip. He looked up and saw her eyes were open.

"Hello, trouble..." she whispered, her voice cracked and sore.

He smiled. "Mum. You're tired – you can sleep."

"I'm OK," she said softly. "Better now you're here." She turned her head slightly and looked up at Dad. "Now you're both here."

Dad leant forward and kissed her head. "We're not going anywhere."

They all stayed like that. Her eyes fluttering as if she was fighting sleep. Occasionally she would smile. The room was silent apart from the gentle rattle and assorted beeps of the oxygen machine.

"Alfie. How was your last match?" she asked finally. "Did you win?"

"Yeah, five-two. I scored three," he said, grinning.

"I'm so proud of you..." she said, then she paused, swallowed hard. "You are amazing, do you know that?"

"Mum..."

"When's your next game?"

"Saturday. It's our last game of the season."

She managed a small smile. "You have to go."

He stared at her. Saturday was only a few days away, but he was scared. Every time he saw her she seemed to be getting weaker and weaker. This was an away match;

he'd be gone for most of the day. Surely it wouldn't be right to be there instead of with her.

"I'll be fine," she said, as if reading his mind. "I'm not going anywhere. I want you to play."

"Mum. . ." He gripped her hand tighter. "I want to stay with you."

"I know. I know you do." She breathed in hard. "I want to be with you. And I still will be. I'll be there on the sidelines . . . cheering you on. I'll be there, Alfie. Just think of me. I'll be there."

He squeezed her hand, not able to reply. He nodded numbly.

"I'll always be there. . ." she whispered, as sleep took hold of her once again.

Chapter Nineteen

I walked over to Alice's feeling quite excited even though I wasn't sure what she was planning for us to do. It was a nice afternoon: the sun was out and trying its best to cast its weak rays down on me, despite it being November. The sky had a cool blue look. Everything seemed fresher and brighter.

As I walked I decided to call Ben. I felt a bit guilty for blowing him out before.

"All right!" he said. "What you been up to?"

"Not much. Went to a game just now with my dad."

There was a pause while Ben obviously considered this. "That's good, isn't it?"

"Yeah, I guess it is."

Ben spoke again. "Look, mate. I know we're two different people. Total opposites, really. I'm not expecting you to wanna be part of my world or anything. . ."

"We're not *that* different," I said, even though I kind of knew he was right.

"I just want you to be OK. You've had a rough ride. You should get out more, you know?"

"I'm actually going out right now," I said, hardly believing it myself.

Ben laughed. "Nice one. What, with the footie lads?"

"No, with Alice – the girl I told you about. She's all right, you know. She's quite a laugh."

I could almost hear Ben nodding. "Fair enough. But you shouldn't blow off Cole and the rest of them though. I know they've been idiots – well, they *are* idiots at times – but I think he feels bad about stuff. I think he misses you too."

"Yeah, *course* he does. . ." I couldn't hide the sarcasm.

"Alf. I know you miss the football. And you can't use Cole as an excuse for ever. You *are* allowed to enjoy the game again, you know? You might actually find that it helps."

I didn't answer. Just kept walking, trying to ignore the burn in my cheeks.

"Your mum loved you playing. She'd hate to see you give it all up."

"I know you're trying to help, mate," I said softly. "I am thinking about taking up training again. You know, just starting off slowly."

"That's good, you really should," Ben replied firmly. "I just want you to be happy. I want you back doing what you're good at." He paused. "You know I've always got your back, don't you? I'm *always* here if you *do* need a mate, albeit a slightly weird one." His tone changed. It was more serious now. "If what happened to your mum teaches you anything, let it be that life is bloody short. We shouldn't waste it."

"Are you going to stop lecturing me now?"

He sniggered. "Yeah, you loser, why not? Just as long as you start enjoying yourself again."

I buzzed the doorbell and waited. The house was quieter this time and that made it seem even bleaker somehow, almost drenched in darkness. I waited there for a while, and started to wonder if anyone was actually in, when—

"Hello?" said her throaty voice over the intercom.

"Alice. It's Alfie."

"Alfie?" There was a pause. "You're early – I didn't expect you for another hour or so."

I glanced at my phone. Five o'clock. To be fair Alice hadn't specified an actual time before, I'd just assumed that she'd want to get out of the house as soon as possible. The sun was shining. What was stopping us?

"It's OK," she said, as if she'd read my thoughts. "Come on up."

She buzzed me in.

Their door was open when I got to the top of the stairs, and Alice was standing just behind it. For once she had her hair scraped up in a messy bun. She looked different without it wild and messy around her face. She was still dressed in PJs.

Seriously? Most of the day had gone already.

"Hey, sorry I came so early," I said, feeling a bit awkward.

"Nah, its OK. It's just I need to get ready, have a shower and that. It's only me and Henry here. Mum's taken the baby out for a walk."

I nodded and walked into the room. I'd forgotten how small it was, and I couldn't help thinking about how hard it must be for an entire family to squeeze into this tiny space. Poor Henry looked like he was fighting for room on the unmade bed; his eyes were glued on the mini TV in the corner.

"Hi!" I said to him. I tried to sound friendly but I wasn't used to being around young kids.

Henry looked up and a smile took over his entire face. "Can you play with me?" he asked straight away.

"Henry!" Alice exclaimed as she stepped between us. "Alfie isn't here to play with you."

"I don't mind," I said, even though I kind of did. I just wanted to be nice.

"Can you . . . can you play football with me?" said Henry, bouncing on the bed.

"Well, I. . ."

"Actually, could you, Alfie?" said Alice, her expression all serious. "There's a shared garden out the back, they even have a little goal there. Mum just doesn't like him going out on his own."

"I'm a stranger to him," I said lamely.

"But I know you," Alice said. "Please, I can follow you out once I've had a quick shower. Henry's going stir-crazy in here."

I sighed. "Have you got a ball?" I asked.

"Yes I do!" Henry shrieked, and he ran off to rummage in a box before coming back, clutching a bright red tatty football. I shrugged, fighting back the grin that threatened to appear.

"OK then. But prepare to be beaten!"

The last time I'd touched a ball had been at the match back in early May. That probably wouldn't sound like long to most people, but to me it felt like a lifetime. Up until then I'd been kicking balls around for as long as I could remember. And now here I was, standing on the patio of some strange garden with a kid I barely knew.

Henry took the ball first and punted it across the grass. I tried not to cringe – he was young and obviously hadn't been taught what to do and how to do it properly.

"You need to kick it like this," I said. "Don't use your toes, use the side of your foot."

I placed the ball on the ground and kicked with my instep, watching as it lifted smoothly into the air and landed sweetly in the back of the shaggy goal at the end of the garden.

"Wow!" Henry said, jumping up and down. "You kicked that really far."

I stared at the ball nestling at the back of the frayed net. I had forgotten how satisfying it felt to do something that I was truly good at. I had forgotten all of this.

I got Henry practising, showing him how to lift the ball with his foot, how to kick it smoothly, how to drag it back away from a potential attacker. For a kid, he was a quick and fast learner.

"You should join a team," I told him.

"Really?" His eyes were wide.

"Yeah, sure. You're good enough." I thought about it for a second. Cookbridge had a younger side. Henry would fit in well there. "I'll tell your mum about a team I know. They'd love to have you."

"Is it your team?"

"Ye— nah. . ." I shook my head. "It's my old team."

I kicked the ball around aimlessly.

"Do you have a new team?" he said, his voice bright and curious.

I paused. "No. . ." I said finally.

"But you're so good!"

I grinned at him. I couldn't believe how good such a simple comment made me feel.

"Can you do keepie-uppies?" he asked.

"Sure."

"How many?"

I frowned. It had been a while – I didn't even know if I could do it any more. "I dunno . . . twenty?"

"Twenty!" he shrieked. "Show me – please."

It wasn't the best ball. A bit flat, a bit old, but I controlled it quite easily. I went into my sort of trance-like state, concentrating hard as I bounced the ball from foot to foot. Under my breath I counted, but I needn't have bothered – Henry was shouting out numbers in front of me.

1, 2, 3. . .

He watched me avidly, his smile growing. I really liked him. He reminded me a bit of what I used to be like when I was little. When I used to drag Dad outside to practise skills with. The ball moved effortlessly from foot to foot. Every so often I'd flip it against my leg. On to my chest, still keeping it in the air – my focus fixed.

23, 24, 25. . .

I had forgotten about those times. Dad and me, every weekend, practising together. He had been there encouraging me, making me better. Then we would go home and report my progress to Mum, and she would be so pleased. Hearing about it would always make her smile. "I love seeing you two happy."

42, 43, 44...

That's what she used to say. All the time. How had I forgotten that?

53, 54, 55...

I wondered if Dad had forgotten that too. What would Mum think if she saw us now? Were we letting her down by just giving this all up? I shuddered and lost concentration, watching as the ball bounced away and fell against the patio.

"Wow. That was impressive," I turned and saw Alice standing behind us. She was wearing jeans and a tiny white top. Her hair was loose and wet around her face. She looked like she'd literally just jumped out of the shower.

"You're really good," she said, nodding at me.

"I used to be," I said automatically, as I booted the ball across the garden.

Alice stared at me pointedly. "No, Alfie – you still are. Any idiot can see that."

Charlotte walked next to him as they were leaving, like a comforting shadow guiding them down the corridor.

"We have rooms ready for both of you," she said to his dad. "You might want to think about staying over soon."

He looked up and saw his dad nod, his face pressed into a frown.

"Some people prefer to be here. To be close by, towards the end. . ." she said, her voice trailing off.

"The end."

The words hung between them.

He turned them over in his head. It made him think of when Mum had read to him when he was small. They would be curled up together on his bed, cosy and warm as she read out the words in her sing-song voice – making them come alive somehow. And then she would bang the book shut with a quick, "Off to sleep now."

As they neared the hospice exit, his dad stopped suddenly. "I'm sorry," he mumbled, "I need the toilet." His voice sounded strange and muffled and his cheeks were red. He stumbled off before they could reply.

Charlotte nodded and gestured towards an open door on her left. "This is our family room," she said gently. "You can come here anytime you need some space." He walked into the room automatically. Soft lighting made it feel warm and safe. There were sofas along two of the walls. It was . . . nice.

"Can I leave you here for a moment?" Charlotte asked. "Just for a minute or so? I want to check on your mum again."

He nodded. He had wanted to say, "My mum isn't there – that isn't her lying there on the bed." But his words were trapped inside him. He watched as Charlotte left, closing the door softly behind her, and he felt himself sag. He wanted to sit, or maybe even lay on one of the sofas. He felt so tired. But he was also so restless. Adrenalin was still pushing through his body. He walked to the corner of the room, where a small table stood, with three candles placed on it, all set in a row. He read the small printed sign next to it:

"Light a candle for the one you love."

He thought of his mum. He thought of the woman he

knew, funny, bright. Alive – in every sense of the word. His hand shook as he reached for the lighter that was there. He couldn't just light one candle. He had to light all three. She deserved that.

"Please be OK, Mum," he whispered towards the flickering flame.

"Please don't leave me."

Chapter Twenty

We left Alice's before her Mum came home. Their neighbour Nina had offered to look after Henry, which Alice had only been too pleased to accept.

"He likes it with Nina," she told me. "She has a little girl the same age and they play together. Besides, I could do without seeing Mum when we get back – she'll only give me the third degree about what we're doing. It's nothing to do with her."

We headed over to town. Alice said she was hungry and wanted to get something to eat and I was happy to go along with that. To be fair, we didn't seem to have any better plans.

Alice was carrying her huge bag as always, but this time she was wearing boots rather than her usual trainers. She struggled to walk fast in them, and kept wobbling slightly, like they were too big for her. I grabbed her arm the first couple of times, but she waved me off after that.

"You don't have to worry about me," she said. Her eyes fixed on mine for a moment and then moved away. But I could see something in her gaze. Something softer. Sadder even. She seemed different today.

"I went to a match with my dad today," I told her.

She sniffed. "Really? Sounds nice."

I stuffed my hands deeper into my pockets. "Do you know what? It really was. It felt – I dunno – normal."

"That's good then?"

I nodded. "I guess."

Alice slowed her pace a little. "It was nice of him to take you. My dad would never have taken me anywhere. Well, maybe the pub. But I'd just be sat outside with a packet of crisps and a Coke, while he went in to see his mates."

I frowned. "Seriously? He did that."

"Yeah, quite a bit." She sucked in her cheeks. "I don't see him any more. He wasn't very nice to be around. Got drunk and stuff, you know? So we moved out of his place when I was still little. Then Mum met Ross. . ."

I turned to face her. "I take it he was no better?"

She half laughed. "You could say that. He was amazing at the start. Then Henry came along and the baby and then. . ." She shuddered. "To be honest I'd rather not talk about it."

"That's OK," I said softly.

"But it's good about your dad – it sounds like he's really trying." Her eyes widened. "You should be grateful."

"Yeah . . . yeah I am."

The thing was, I had only just realized how much I was. Because without Dad where would I be?

I'd have nothing left at all.

We carried on walking at a slower pace.

"How long do you think you'll be in the bedsit?" I asked.

Alice made a snorting noise. "My mum is down the council every day begging them. But there are loads of us."

I frowned. "Doesn't that mean they're more likely to get a place for you?"

"It means," sighed Alice, "that bigger houses are harder to come by. And do you know what's worse? Half the houses on our road look like they're empty. Great big houses with no one is living inside them owned by rich people that can afford second homes to use two weeks a year on holiday. How can that be right?"

I shook my head. I couldn't answer that. I'd wasted time moaning about the fact that Dad and me were rattling around inside our house, but that was what Alice wanted more than anything. Not even wanted – needed.

"I'm sorry. I shouldn't be ranting at you," she muttered. "It just gets to me. The world seems so wrong sometimes."

"No, it's OK. I get it."

"You must feel so much worse – I mean, you must feel so upset about your mum. I can't even imagine what that's like. I'm going off on one about a stupid house when you've lost her. I'm sorry. That was out of order."

I screwed up my face as I tried to think. I wanted to be able to answer this.

"I feel lots of things. Upset, yeah, but angry too. Angry that the cancer won – that she couldn't fight it any more, that she let it beat her. Even though I know that's wrong of me. I know I shouldn't think that, because she fought for as long as she could."

"I understand that, totally," Alice said softly.

"Do you?"

"Yeah, course. I think I'd be angry too."

I blinked and exhaled slowly. It really helped that she'd said that. It made a difference somehow.

"I feel guilty too," I said. "I have this horrible, sick guilt that won't go away."

"Why?" she asked, her voice still soft.

"Because. . . Because I can't act like I used to. I can't pretend that everything is all right. How can I go back to how I used to be? Playing football, being with those lads. The last time I did that. The last time I tried to pretend everything was OK. . ."

We stopped walking, and Alice turned to face me. She looked really serious as her eyes fixed on mine. She took my hand.

"No one is asking you to pretend, Alfie. Obviously I didn't know your mum, but she wouldn't want you to feel like this, would she? She wouldn't want you beating yourself up."

"I feel like I let her down. . ." I said, barely able to get the words out. My voice broke with the weight of my confession. I'd never said it out loud before. I turned my face away so she couldn't see my tears.

"No. No you didn't, Alfie," she said as she squeezed

my hand. "OK, I don't know everything that went on, but I think I know you well enough now and I know you didn't let her down. But to be honest, I think you are now – you're letting her down by thinking like this."

"I want to make her happy."

"Then stop hurting yourself. Stop living in the past." Alice said gently. "You can't bring her back, Alfie. You can never do that. But you can live the life she wanted you to live."

I sniffed and nodded, feeling a bit pathetic. But as we started walking again, I noticed that the heavy rock that used to sit in my stomach felt different.

It felt lighter.

We sat on the beach again, further down this time, on the last bit of the stones before they got wet from the raging tide. It was so cold from the now biting wind. I pulled my hood up over my ears and tried to ignore the icy blast. It didn't seem to be bothering Alice at all. She simply sat quietly cross-legged, facing the sea.

"It's so angry today," she said.

I looked out at the crashing waves, turning and tumbling in quick succession.

"Imagine being out in it, being swept away in that cold water. How long would it take before. . ."

The words caught in her throat. She didn't say any more. Instead her fingers skimmed the rocks.

Until what? Until you drowned? Until you closed your eyes and it was all over?

I'd thought about it before of course. I'd come down here by myself. I'd stood by the railings and looked out at that grey, unforgiving water and wondered if I should do it, just close my eyes and jump in.

Would it stop the hurting? Would the pain stop?

"It would be awful," Alice said finally, her voice firm and brittle. "It would be the worst thing to die like that."

I nodded. "Yeah it would."

"Sometimes I think stuff like that, but I don't really mean it. I just wonder. That's all." Her voice drifted again. "Sometimes I just want to stop hurting – you know?"

"Yeah. I know."

She flinched. "You do?"

"I wonder about it sometimes too. Dying," I said, my eyes still fixed on the sea. "But I've seen death face on. I've seen what it does to people. To everyone else that's left behind." I paused. "It's never worth giving up, is it? I mean, my mum, she fought so hard to stay alive. She fought for her life. I could never just throw it away. It's too precious."

Alice looked at me, and I mean she really looked at me. It was like she could see me for the first time. "Yes," she said. "Yes. It is. When Mum first met Ross, it was good," she said softly. "She was so happy and that made me happy. We never really saw my Dad any more, which was a good thing I guess. But Mum was lonely and so was I really – I wanted that sort of person in my life." She shuddered a little. "Ross seemed to be perfect. He made Mum smile, he was lovely to me – buying presents and that, even though I wasn't his kid."

"But he's Henry and Amy's Dad?" I asked.

Alice nodded. "Yeah. Yeah he is. It was after Henry was born that Ross started to change. He seemed to get angry at Mum for no reason. He hated the baby crying too much. He'd have a go about the house looking a mess and stuff like that. I mean, it was his house, so Mum always seemed to be stressed out about keeping it clean. I used to have to help her, even though I was only little myself." She sighed, pushing back a strand of hair. "I heard her crying a lot, when I was in bed, and him shouting. He did that a lot. He called her names, he laughed at her. . ."

I frowned. That sounded awful. "And you said he hurt her too."

Alice picked up a stone and gripped it in her hands. "Yeah. He did. He hit her. But he was nasty too; he hurt her worse with his words. He'd take the mickey out of her – say that she was pathetic and no one else would want her. One time, Mum told him she was going to leave him – that was in front of me – and Ross just laughed in her face. He said if she ever left, he would find her. He would make her life hell."

"Oh, Alice. . ." I didn't know what to say.

"She took us, one night. We crept out while he was round some mate's. This was even before Amy was born. We ended up at some hostel somewhere. But he found us. He told Mum to stop being stupid and made us come home." She threw the rock along the beach. "Mum said he had a way of getting inside her head, of making her think that she was the one to blame – that she had done something wrong. We must have left him four or five times, but he still found us. He still got us back."

"Except now," I said.

Alice turned to me, and her eyes were sparkling with tears. "Mum took a call earlier today. She thinks I didn't hear her but I did. She was talking to him. Someone has given Ross her number and now he will get back inside her head – he will find out where we are living now." Her voice wobbled. "She couldn't even look me in the eye when she went out earlier. Maybe she even met up with him, who knows?" She shrugged. "Either way I know she'll either go back to him or make us run away again. We can't stay here now he's found us. He will hurt her, really hurt her this time. . ."

"Can't you talk to her?" I asked. "Can't you tell her how you're feeling?"

Alice smirked. "Listen to you. Now you're the expert on communication." She paused. "I've tried telling her before, but she never listens to me."

"So what will you do now?"

Alice turned away from me again, her eyes fixed back on the sea. "I'll go with her wherever she wants. She needs me. We'll do what we always do – keep moving, keep running, keep hiding."

I reached forward and touched her arm, gently squeezed it. This all seemed so wrong. Both of us had been pushed into directions we didn't want to go in, and yet what other option did we have but to ride the storm and hope that it burnt itself out quickly?

"I'll miss you if you go," I said.

I felt her shake a little under my grip. "I'll miss you too, loser."

Dad couldn't come. He understood – of course he did – but him not being there made it so much harder. It was bad enough not having Mum on the side-lines.

"Go, son. Please. Nothing will change," Dad had said. "I just think one of us needs to be with her."

"I could stay," he'd said. He actually didn't want to go. He felt so tired. His head hurt and his mind was too busy thinking of other things. How could he concentrate on the game?

"Some time away from here might help you. And it's your last match of the season – an important one. Don't let them down." Dad had squeezed his shoulder. "Mum wants you to go."

Mum. She said she'd be there with him. But she wouldn't, would she? Not really. She wouldn't be yelling his name, jumping up and down and embarrassing him by squealing every time he got tackled.

Granddad drove him to the grounds but he could barely talk. He pressed his face up against the window and watched the world blur in a hazy rush. That was what his life felt like, he realized: a blur. Everything was moving too fast. He wasn't in control. It was like being in this car, but going much, much faster, racing down a motorway, with everything he loved being left behind.

He couldn't make it stop. However hard he tried, he couldn't stop it, or even slow down what was happening.

Granddad spoke to him as he put on his boots and went to join the others, but he barely noticed. Walking over to his teammates, he felt heavy and slow. He prayed that Mum would be awake when he got back, so that he could tell her all about the game. He could score an amazing goal and replay it for her. That would cheer her up.

The thought of this made him happier.

They warmed up. Cole and the others were in good moods.

"I know you've got stuff going on," said Cole, "but we've got to win today. Try to stay focused."

Cole thought he knew everything. It was irritating, but he swallowed it down. He didn't need any more anger. He had enough burning inside.

The match was about to start. They were playing

Heathfield, their main rivals. A few of the players made some jeery comments but he ignored them, concentrating on jogging on the spot. His gaze drifted to far side where the small collection of parents stood huddled together. He could see Granddad at the far end, but he also saw the gaping space next to him.

His mind wandered. How was she?

The whistle blew and he started to move automatically, following the action. He was out wide on the left and most of the play was concentrated in the centre to begin with. For a while he had little to do but follow his marker. But then Cole intercepted a pass and Alfie spotted a chance to break, leaving his marker yards behind him.

"Cole!" he yelled, pointing in front of him.

Cole spotted him and lofted the ball sweetly. With one touch, Alfie brought the ball down on his left instep without breaking his stride. He surged down the line and realized the central defender was coming across to cover. The boy who came rushing towards him was clumsy and playing out of position. Desperate to get the ball, the gangly defender made a last-minute decision to slide tackle him, taking his feet clear off the ground.

Alfie was lifted briefly into the air. And then he fell hard on to the baked mud. His ankle twisted awkwardly beneath him. His body exploded in shock.

The boy ran over and tried to pull him up. "I'm sorry," he gasped. "You're just so fast."

He jumped up, the pain in his ankle screaming. This had been his chance, his last chance to make his mum proud. He gripped the other player's shirt, pulling him in.

"You idiot. You stupid idiot," he screamed. "I was clear." He was shaking with rage.

"Mate . . . come on." It was Cole, trying to break it up, trying to gently pull him away.

But he'd shaken Cole off. "Leave it!" he'd screamed.

Cole had tried again. Pulling him harder now. "Alfie, you need to come off. We need to look at your ankle."

"Get off me. I'm still playing!"

"No, mate. No you're not." Cole turned to the other boy. "I'm sorry, he's a bit wound up at the moment. His mum's not well."

Wound up? As if Cole knew anything about being wound up. As if Cole knew anything about any of it. And how dare he talk about his mum to a complete stranger?

The punch landed on Cole's chin before he even knew what was going on. It was a hard blow and it sent him flying to the floor, a shocked expression on his face.

But he deserved it.

He shoved past his coach who had run over too late,

shoved past the other players who were standing there in frozen confusion.

"Take me to Mum," he said to his granddad. "Please."

They drove back to the hospice, his granddad driving quickly, knowing that he needed him to. But when they reached the main drive, he could sense something was wrong. A sense of dread washed over him.

He got out of the car and ran, leaving his granddad behind, still wearing his boots and full kit. He raced through the hallway towards her room. And he knew. He knew.

A nurse – a different one – was coming out of the door. She was small and pretty, with a kind smile.

"Alfie?" she said, somehow knowing who he was.

He nodded.

They walked in and he saw his dad's white face, how he was gripping her limp hand while staring off into space. Then he saw her. His mum. Her eyes tightly closed, her mouth open, her tiny body fighting for breath.

"Is she dying?" he whispered. It was the question that had been trapped inside him for so long now.

"It won't be long now, Alfie," said Dad. "She's nearly ready to let go."

She was leaving them. This was the beginning of the end.

Chapter Twenty-one

We walked back home in near silence. I think both of us were so tired, so beyond talking. My head was full of my own thoughts – decisions rattling through me. Suddenly everything was becoming so much clearer. I knew what I had to do now.

It was what Alice had said earlier – "I have to keep on moving" – that had settled in my own brain and made so much sense. I had to do the same. I couldn't stay like this – frozen, too scared to move forward. Too scared to be myself again. I had to keep pressing on. It was the only way.

Alice had helped me realize that.

I saw the police car outside her house before she did. I stopped in my tracks, my words frozen in my throat. Behind me I heard Alice suck in her breath.

"No!"

"It might not be to do with you," I reasoned. She lived in a shared house after all; they could be there for any one of the families that lived there.

Alice didn't move behind me. "No. I know it's for us. It's Ross. I just know it. He's hurt her."

She ran then, suddenly, taking me by surprise. She was really quick and got up to the front door in seconds, her hair more wild than ever – her finger punching the buttons.

"Let me in!" she yelled into the intercom.

I came up behind her, feeling awkward and useless. Tentatively I touched her shoulder and wasn't surprised when she flinched under me.

"Alice – don't panic."

"It wasn't Mum who answered our number!" she said, her eyes wild. "I don't know who it was!"

We both waited as the front door swung open and a police officer stepped out to meet us. She held out her hand to Alice.

"Alice. Are you Alice Jenkins?"

Alice nodded numbly.

"Alice – we were worried about you."

Alice pushed her hair out of her face. "Where's my mum?"

"She's fine. She's upstairs waiting for you. But she didn't know where you were. She's been very concerned."

Alice just shrugged. "I didn't think she'd be bothered. She knows I go out."

"I hear you've been doing this a bit too often recently," the police officer said softly. "And your Mum does worry. Especially now. . ."

Alice stiffened. "Especially now, why?" Her voice dropped, barely a whisper. "It's Ross, isn't it? He's found us?"

The police officer's smile was a gentle one. Slowly she nodded. "Yes, we have reason to suspect he has." She paused. "And he told your mum you were with him. That's why she was so frantic."

I'd never seen Alice look so pale. "He must've been watching me. He must have seen me leave the house."

The officer gently took Alice's arm. "You need to come inside. We all need to talk. There's a lot we need to sort out."

I watched as they walked inside. I knew that they had stuff to sort out and this had nothing to do with me, but I was still sad. I still felt guilty that I couldn't help Alice more.

"*Please don't leave,*" I whispered into the wind.

And then I turned around and headed back home.

I needed my dad.

He was in the kitchen when I walked in, making tea and singing softly under his breath. For a few seconds I just stood and watched him. My dad.

Mine

Where would I have been without him? Despite everything. Despite the fact that he hadn't spoken to me enough about Mum, that he had seemed to push me away – he'd still always been here. He'd been a constant in my life. And I needed him so much. I knew this now.

"Alfie?" He turned to face me, looking confused. "Are you OK?"

"I guess." I slumped myself down on the nearest chair and slowly told him about Alice. About Ross and her mum and how scared she had seemed.

Dad breathed out hard. "Wow. Poor girl."

"I just feel so bad. I didn't realize how rough she had it. . ." I squeezed my hands into a fist. "I was so caught up in my own stuff."

Dad was facing me with an intense look on his face. He seemed so sad.

"Do you think she'll be OK?" I asked.

He sat down on the chair opposite me, his hand rubbing his face. "I think so. You say the police are involved now, so hopefully they will help. Hopefully they can help her and her mum."

"I reckon they will move away again."

Dad sighed. "It's not right, is it? Why should they have to keep moving because of some . . . some monster?"

I shook my head. "I don't want her to have to move again. She's just getting settled here. It's not fair."

Dad reached forward and took my hand. "She'll be OK, son. Whatever happens, she'll be OK. And she'll be thankful to have a friend like you around."

"Some friend. . ." I muttered. After all, what did I do?

"Of course you are! You've been there for her. You listened to her. That's probably what she needs right now."

I shrugged. "I guess."

"I don't tell you this often enough, Alfie, but I'm proud of you."

I looked up. Stared right up at my Dad. "Eh?"

Dad's eyes were glassy, and he squeezed my hand tight. "Seriously? How could I not be proud? These past few months you've been like a rock soldiering on. And now this, helping someone out again. Putting someone before yourself. I don't know – I really don't know how you've been coping so well since your mum died, without any counselling, without any help – you're so strong. . ."

Coping? Strong? Was he for real?

But Dad wasn't finished. He suddenly got up, walked over and then crouched down beside me. I have never known him to do anything that intimate before.

"You were strong, right up until the end. Right where I couldn't be. I'm ashamed, Alfie. I'm ashamed that I froze, that I couldn't do anything to help your mum – but you, you were different. You knew just what to do – you held her hand, you said the right things – you. . .

He choked. Paused. His hand flew up to his mouth. "You helped her, right at the end, when I was so bloody useless."

I shook my head. I couldn't hear this. But Dad kept on.

"But then I've started to see that you're not

managing, are you? Not really? You're building up big walls. You're blocking everyone out. Stopping football, pushing your friends away. You're doing all this stupid stuff as a way to escape the reality, the truth."

I couldn't answer; I just kept staring at him. I could feel my whole body tense and then start to shake.

"Do you know how I know this?" he said. "It's because it's exactly what I'm doing too. I can't stand the fact that your mum has gone, so I pack it away. I try not deal with it. I try to pretend like everything is still OK, and it's killing me—"

His voice broke. I looked at him. He was crying.

Proper crying.

"I'm so sorry, Alfie," he sobbed. "I've let you down. I should have been here for you. Instead I've just left you to get on. I thought it was better – I thought it would be best for you not seeing me like this – but now – now, I think I got it wrong..."

The shaking was taking over me. I opened my mouth to speak, but there was nothing I could say. We were done talking. Instead, I reached forward, folded myself into his arms. He took hold of me, really grabbed me like he was scared I would run away, and pressed me against his chest. I could feel him shaking too. He nestled his head in my hair and sobbed once again.

But this time they were huge, ugly sobs.

I didn't even know I was doing it too, until I realized that my tears were soaking his shirt.

We stayed like that for ages.

It was the only thing left to do.

Afterwards we sat together. Dad made us both tea and even though I hadn't drunk the stuff for years, I really enjoyed it. It seemed to warm me up from inside.

"We are going to start going to games again," Dad said softly. "We are going to spend that time together. We need to do it. We need to get some kind of normality back."

I nodded. OK. That sounded good.

"And..." Dad hesitated. I could see he was struggling to speak. "And ... there's a woman at the hospice. We can both speak to her. It might help us ... you know. It might help us deal with this all better." He paused again. "Can you try it? I mean – if I do, will you?"

I gulped the tea. Blinked hard.

"Yeah..." I said. "I guess I can try."

Dad nodded. "Good."

"And Dad?" I put my mug back down on the table. "I think I want to go back to training again."

His eyes glistened, and a small smile crept up on his face. "Really? Are you sure?"

"Yeah..." I smiled back. "I'd like to."

Dad reached across and took my hand in his. Squeezed it tight. "I think that would be amazing," he said. "I just want to see you happy again."

"I want us both to be happy."

"And we will, son," he whispered in a voice I barely recognized. "Small steps, but we will get there. We have each other."

Yeah.

That was the one thing we did have left. And I was going to hold on hard to it.

I knew how precious it was.

Alice came over the next day. She looked different. Thinner, paler and her face was un-made-up. It was strange seeing her eyes without the heavy dark liner.

"I wanted to thank you," she said softly.

"I didn't do anything," I replied.

She smiled at me shyly. "You listened to me rant for most of the afternoon and then you made sure I got home OK ... so you did a lot. A lot more than most would, anyway."

"Do you want come in?" I asked her.

"No ... it's OK. I can't stay long." Her arms were hanging loosely by her sides. "I just wanted to see you quickly."

My stomach twisted. "Are you all right? Are you leaving again?"

Alice grinned. "Would you miss me if I did?"

I could feel my cheeks redden. "Well ... yes of course, a bit." I paused. "You're my mate. Of course I'd miss you."

"I'd miss you too." She said. "But it's OK. You don't have to panic, we're not going anywhere. Well, not far anyway. Mum went to the police yesterday about Ross, she asked for their help. The police are now going to help Mum serve Ross an injunction which means he can't go anywhere near us or he'll get arrested."

"Nice one." I nudged her. "So I'm stuck with you for a bit longer then?"

She lifted her head. A small smile settled on her face. "You know, I liked you the minute I first saw you. Standing there talking to the dumb birds. I just knew you were different. You were someone who was really *feeling* something." She shook her head. "I try so hard not to feel, because all I get is hurt and pain and I can't stand it."

"I totally get that."

"You get it more than most, Alfie. You lost your mum. And there I was whinging about my problems. It's so lame." She moved away from me. "I'm sorry. I'm sorry I dragged you into my mess yesterday."

I shivered. Her words struck a chord. But was she right? We both had our problems and we both struggled dealing with them.

But it felt like my life was fixing itself. I was no longer a mess of missing parts.

"Will you be OK?" I asked her.

She stared back at me. I'd never realized how clear blue her eyes were, like tiny pools of ice. "I'm going to be fine. I don't feel as scared now. I finally believe Mum when she says she won't go back to him. She seems different. She seems stronger now, like she actually knows she can do this without him." Alice smiled softly and scuffed the ground with her feet. "She's also speaking to the council tomorrow. Apparently a place has come up across town. We're first on the list so we can go to view it. She wants us to make this place our home."

I grinned. "That's great news. Will you be far away though?"

"Not so far that I can't still annoy you." Her eyes twinkled. "But it's a relief. It's a chance to start again, you know?"

I knew. I knew all right.

"What are you doing later?" she asked.

"I'm meeting Cole tonight, not seen him for a while and he's going to fill me in on the footie news. But I might take a walk first."

She nodded, a slight smile on her face. "To the beach?"

"Yeah. I kind of need to."

"Will you be OK?" she asked softly.

I looked her straight in the eye. "Yeah – I reckon I will be."

She laughed. It was light and sweet and made me feel happy.

"See you later then, loser?" There was a slight inflection there. I saw her eyes widen and I realized she was asking a question. I was pleased.

"Yeah – I reckon you will..." I said. Then I grabbed a pen that was lying on the table by the door. I lifted her hand and wrote my number carefully on her skin. "Don't wash it off. Maybe you could text me later. We can meet up again." I paused. "I need to introduce you to my mate, Ben. I've got a feeling you two will get on."

She grinned. "Yeah . . . maybe we will."

And then she turned and walked off down the path.

But this time I didn't feel alone.

A little later I found myself standing under the lightning tree. It was late afternoon but the sky was bright against the grey sea. The seagulls squealed above my head. The beach had never looked so peaceful.

I was alone.

But I needed to be.

A seagull swooped down and perched inches away from me on the railings. Its beady eyes stared intently at me, taking me in. I smiled back. He looked familiar somehow.

"All right, mate?"

The bird tipped his head like he was listening, then gave a throaty cry and took flight again, brushing over the top of my head. I thought of Alice. I thought of her taking the mickey out of me for talking to the birds again and I had to fight back a grin.

I took a deep breath in and sucked the sour salty air deep into my lungs, just like Mum used to. I liked the fresh feeling that drifted down my body, seeping through my muscles and boring deep into my bones. It was a strength I wanted. I stared out beyond me, to that familiar sight of the long stretched-out pier.

If I concentrated hard enough, I could almost feel her next to me, here on the beach itself. Her face screwed up in deep thought, her lips locked in a smile, her hair whipping wildly in the breeze.

"I'll always be with you, Alfie..."

Because of course she was. She *always* was.

I just had to remember to look for her.

I just had to remember.

He was sleeping. They had been here for a few days now, sleeping by her side in small pull-up beds. Sleep came in short, restless bursts. Then his eyes would snap open and he would sit up. Make sure he could still hear the sigh of the oxygen machine that told him she was still there. It hadn't ended yet.

Memories that he thought had been long forgotten now fought for attention in his mind while his mum's voice – her laughter, her singing, everything – played on a mental loop. He thought about the sadder times, when she had first been ill. When they had argued. When she had burst into tears for no reason in front of Eastenders. When she had sat just staring out of the window, too cold and weak to go outside. When they lost each other in the market. He had been five or so and had spent ages wandering up and down looking for her. He had been sobbing, thinking she had run away and left him for good. But then she'd appeared, angry that he had run off but so relieved to have found him. She had squeezed him so tightly she took the breath out of him. "Never leave me like that, never. Never."

And he didn't. Not again.

He dreamt he was on a boat. The waves crashing against the wooden sides, and his mum watching from the shore, waving at him. She was getting smaller as his boat drifted further and further away, until he could barely see her.

"Alfie. Alfie. You need to wake up. . ."

Charlotte was shaking his shoulder gently. She was so close he could smell her perfume. The room was still dimly lit. He sat up and saw his dad sitting on the edge of Mum's bed stroking her face. His expression was frozen. He didn't look at Alfie.

"She's nearly ready," Charlotte said softly.

He knew he had to be brave. His whole body felt stiff and his hands were shaking, but he made himself get up. He made himself sit on the edge of the bed and take her hand. Her eyes were closed, but he could hear her breathing – rattling in and out of her lungs in irregular bursts. Her tiny body seemed to be working so hard to get that air into her lungs.

"Is she in pain?" he asked.

"She's struggling, Alfie. But you can talk to her. You can tell her you're here."

He nodded. His dad was sitting further back now. He looked like he was in a daze.

"I love you, Mum", he said, as he slowly moved forward. "I love you so much."

Her breathing rattled beneath him, becoming slower. Much slower.

"You can stop fighting, Mum. It's OK. We'll be OK."

He pushed his face against hers, and his tears fell against the white skin of her face, making it look like she'd been crying too.

"I love you," he whispered. "I want you stop hurting. I want you to go."

Then he buried his head in her chest, one hand still stroking her hair. He lay there until his back cramped up and his arm went numb. He lay there with his eyes squeezed tight, no longer aware of time or movement around him – only of his mum and her thin, warm body beneath him.

He never wanted it to end.

He lay there until the rise in her chest stopped and Charlotte gently touched them both.

"She's gone," she said softly.

And everything around him shattered into a million pieces.

Six months later

It was bitterly cold. I puffed out air, watching the vapour stream and curl in front of me. My hands were numb with cold as I rubbed them together. I had to keep moving. I had to keep warm.

Cole had the ball upfront. Although he was fast, the burly central defender blocked his run, sending the ball hurtling back into our half. I raced forward, my eyes fixed on the gobby midfielder who'd been mouthing off before the game. I couldn't let him gain an advantage. The ball fell between us, but I was there first, controlling then sliding it away with my left foot, skipping the incoming tackle in the process.

I ran, the ball still at my feet. I knew only moments remained.

As their right-back closed me down, I did a step-over with my right foot before flicking the ball swiftly inside with the outside of my boot, leaving the defender wrong-footed. As I approached the eighteen yard box, I looked up to see the goal. I knew the central defender would be moving across to cover my run, so without hesitating I launched a bullet with my instep towards the far corner.

Time could've stood still. Maybe it did. Another icy puff of air escaped my lips. Exhausted, I fell to the ground, my knees crunching against the hard surface. But my gaze was still fixed on the goal. I watched as the ball, that beautiful ball, started wide but quickly curved and dipped, spinning beautifully into the top right corner, emitting a satisfying buzz as it spun down the inside of the net.

The keeper didn't stand a chance. He fell backwards, his hands outstretched. He could never have reached it.

The goal was always going to be mine.

The eighty-ninth minute and finally, finally we had broken through. One-nil.

My faced kissed the ground. I couldn't feel anything for a second and then it was although someone had turned the sound on – really loud. They were all screaming.

The lads clambered on top of me, ruffling my hair, tugging my top. I was laughing. I couldn't stop. And then I felt his hand, pulling me up. Cole. He was standing right in front of me, a wide smile stretched across his red face.

"That," he said, "was legendary."

He pulled me against him, into the tightest hug. We both stank of sweat and mud, but neither of us cared. We were laughing too much.

"Thanks, mate."

I turned around. I wanted to see them. Of course they were right there, fighting to stand at the front of barrier. Dad, Alice and Ben – all jumping up and waving. Dad was clutching the dog's lead, trying desperately to stop Poppy running on the pitch to lick me.

I raised my arm, trying not to cry. Not that it would've mattered. Not any more.

I was back.

He was running along the seafront, a bit too fast, but he was so excited. His short, chubby legs were working hard, keen to get close to them. He was barely five years old and he was eager to show them both how well he could do now. In front of him, she stood with her arms outstretched, a grin growing across her bright face.

"Well done, Alfie. You can do it!" she yelled.

Behind her, Dad was laughing. "Careful now!" he called. "You don't want to—"

He heard the words a little too late, and his eyes glimpsed his dad's concerned gaze before his toe caught the crack in the pavement. He felt himself first stagger and then spill forward on to the broken slabs. A sharp sting radiated up his right knee. Tears rimmed his eyes. His mouth opened into a loud, mournful howl.

His mum ran towards him; she was there in seconds.

Tenderly, she scooped him up in her arms and pressed him against the soft material of his dress. She didn't speak, she just made hushing tones under her breath as she gently rocked him.

His dad gently peeled them apart, inspected his knee and then sighed.

"Oh. That looks painful."

He lifted his head and peered towards the knee, and seeing the bubble of blood, he howled again.

"It's only blood, Alfie," his Dad said softly. "It'll be gone soon. It's just there to fix the wound on your knee."

"Is it bad?" he stuttered.

His dad shook his head. "It's not bad at all. You'll get a tiny scab and it'll be gone. You'll forget about it."

"I won't scar like you?"

His dad glanced down at the fine line on arm; silvery and puckered with age it now looked like a faded tattoo. He'd been going too fast on his motorbike. He had been lucky not to lose his arm. He shook his head.

Alfie sat up. Interested now, he gripped his dad's arm and looked again and the shiny white line.

"Does it still hurt?" he asked.

"No. Not now."

"It's horrible."

His dad paused for a moment and then bent down

and kissed him lightly on his head. "It hurt at the time, then it healed a bit. The scar is my reminder. Sometimes you need to remember these things."

"I don't want a scar," he sobbed.

His mum wrapped him back in her arms. "We all have scars. Inside and out. It makes us who we are."

He wasn't sure he understood, but in that moment he wasn't sure it mattered. His dad sat down beside them, took a tissue out of his pocket and gently attempted to remove the tiny stones from his cut. Then carefully he rinsed away the blood with his bottled water. All the time his mum held him and soothed him.

"My knee still hurts," he said after a bit.

His mum simply held him a little closer.

"It'll stop hurting so badly soon." Her words were like a soothing balm, and he began to slowly relax in her arms.

"Just wait and see, Alfie. The pain will ease, I promise you."

He closed his eyes, understanding now. It wouldn't hurt as bad soon.

It just needed time.

The End

Acknowledgements

I have so many people to thank and my brain always goes into panic mode, trying to remember you all. Please be assured that I am always grateful for those around me that have supported me through the grumpy times and encouraged me when I'm feeling deflated. You are the anchors on my very wobbly boat.

As always, I want to thank my wonderful husband, Tom. I'm not usually gushy (as he will testify) but he does deserve a lot of credit for the input he provides. Tom will read my early drafts to check for very silly mistakes, he will keep me buoyant when I'm sinking in self-doubt and he will make me endless cups of tea. Thank you, Tom – I love you and I'm so grateful to have you.

Thank you too, to my children Ella and Ethan for helping with ideas, making me laugh and not killing each other when I was in the midst of writing. You're not bad kids really. I might not sell you on Ebay just yet.

Thank you to my writer friends who always offer such wonderful support. The children's writing community is such a friendly and inclusive one and I feel lucky to be part of it. In particular thank you to Emma, Sarah and Keren for your wise words and for reading my wonky early works. I love you all.

Endless love to my family – you are a wonderful lot. I'm

lucky to have such a large and supportive network. In particular: Mum, Jack, Cherry, Ali, Kate, Dave, Joe, Iain, Simon, David – thank you for listening to me and for putting up with me for so long.

I'm also lucky to have such a good bunch of friends. The Rebels – you know who you are. Keep being awesome, you amazing bunch! Also I'd like to give individual thanks to Amanda and Gemma who have been there when I've needed them the most.

To every librarian out there – I thank you. You change lives and you help so many. I hope to meet many more of you in the coming years.

To every book blogger out there – thank you for all tireless hard work supporting books and reading. You are fabulous!

Lastly, I wouldn't be where I am today without the support of my wonderful agent, Stephanie Thwaites, and my editor, Fiz Osborne. Thank you both for the hard work, wise words and faith in me. I am lucky to have you.

Finally, I want to acknowledge the young boy who I met four years ago. The young boy who had lost his mother and was struggling to deal with his grief. His story never left me and it helped to shape the story that finally became *Lost*. I think of this boy often and I hope that he is in a better place today. I want to thank him for showing me what raw grief in young boys can look like. He was one of the bravest boys I ever met.